Dear Diary,

Hannah called from Seat
the news, and I'm almost
Ben Jessup are an item!

Then again, maybe it's not so strange after all. They're both passionate, committed people, and both have suffered tragedy in their lives.

How ironic that Ben built his house on the same lot in Forrester Square where Alexandra's family lived until the fire that killed her parents and caused the nightmares that haunt her day and night. Or maybe the fact that Ben's there is just a sign that fate is at work for the two of them.

I wish I could tell Alexandra that Dr. Ben Jessup could be her destiny...the man who will love her the way she deserves to be loved.

Or perhaps it's Ben I should warn. Tell him not to give up, no matter how much Alexandra tries to push him away. She's been running all her adult life—from her tragic past, from the nightmares, from herself—and there's nothing to say she won't take off again. But the more I think about it, the more I'm convinced that Ben may well be the safe haven she longs for.

It's been so wonderful working with Alexandra and Hannah this past year. And now that Hannah and I are each married to the man of our dreams and have new paths to follow, we want the same for Alexandra. After all, what happier ending could there be for the three best friends from Forrester Square?

Till tomorrow,

Katherine

JOANNA WAYNE
and her husband live just a few miles from steamy, exciting New Orleans, but their home is the perfect writer's hideaway. A lazy bayou, complete with graceful egrets, colorful wood ducks and an occasional alligator, winds just below her back garden. When not writing, Joanna loves reading, golfing, or playing with her grandchildren, and of course researching and plotting out her next novel of intrigue and passion. She also teaches writing classes at a local university and is active in several writing groups. Writing is a passion for Joanna, second in importance only to her family. Taking the heroine and hero from danger to enduring love and happy-ever-after is all in a day's work for her, and who could complain about a day like that?

Forrester Square

LEGACIES . LIES . LOVE .

JOANNA WAYNE

ESCAPE THE NIGHT

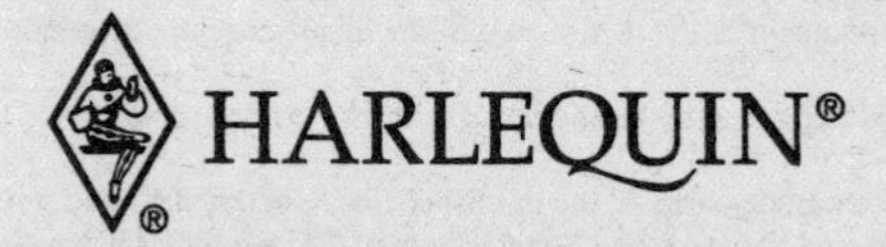

TORONTO • NEW YORK • LONDON
AMSTERDAM • PARIS • SYDNEY • HAMBURG
STOCKHOLM • ATHENS • TOKYO • MILAN • MADRID
PRAGUE • WARSAW • BUDAPEST • AUCKLAND

A special thanks to Jerry and Marilyn Tobolski for their Washington hospitality and for sharing their love of the Seattle area with me. An added thanks to Jerry for answering my endless questions and providing invaluable links to maps and research sources. A special thanks is also due to Marsha Zinberg and her staff for coming up with the idea for such a marvelous series and for being so wonderful to work with. And, always, a kiss to Wayne for having the patience to live with a writer.

HARLEQUIN BOOKS
225 Duncan Mill Road, Don Mills,
Ontario, Canada M3B 3K9

ISBN 0-373-61279-6

ESCAPE THE NIGHT

Joanna Wayne is acknowledged as the author of this work.

This edition published by arrangement with Harlequin Books S.A.

Visit us at www.eHarlequin.com

Printed in U.S.A.

Dear Reader,

Seattle, a mysterious underground, a mystery that spans more than twenty years, breath-stealing suspense and heartwarming romance—what's not to love about a story that involves all these ingredients? Needless to say, I was very excited about the prospect of writing book 12 in the FORRESTER SQUARE series. Since I'd never been to the Seattle area, I decided this was the perfect excuse to make the journey. I went to visit, and fell as much in love with the area as I did with the characters in my story. And, yes, I did get hooked on Seattle coffee, though my favorite was the iced caramel latte.

I love to hear from readers, and you can write me a personal note by visiting my Web site at www.eclectics.com/authorsgalore/joannawayne. Be sure to enter the authors galore contest to win a free book while you're there. Or you can write me at P.O. Box 2851, Harvey, LA 70059-2851 to request a free newsletter and bookmark.

Happy reading,

Joanna Wayne

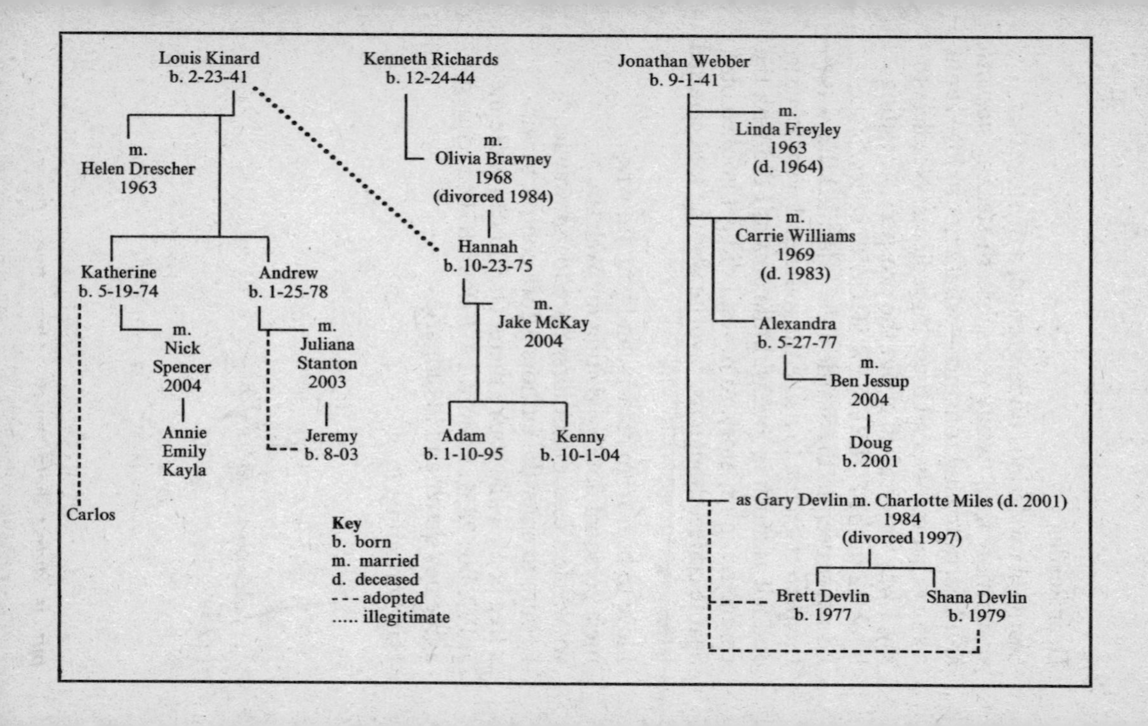

Louis Kinard
b. 2-23-41
m.
Helen Drescher
1963
Katherine
b. 5-19-74
m.
Nick
Spencer
2004
Annie
Emily
Kayla
Carlos
Andrew
b. 1-25-78
m.
Juliana
Stanton
2003
Jeremy
b. 8-03
Kenneth Richards
b. 12-24-44
m.
Olivia Brawney
1968
(divorced 1984)
Hannah
b. 10-23-75
m.
Jake McKay
2004
Adam
b. 1-10-95
Kenny
b. 10-1-04
Jonathan Webber
b. 9-1-41
m.
Linda Freyley
1963
(d. 1964)
m.
Carrie Williams
1969
(d. 1983)
Alexandra
b. 5-27-77
m.
Ben Jessup
2004
Doug
b. 2001
as Gary Devlin m. Charlotte Miles (d. 2001)
1984
(divorced 1997)
Brett Devlin
b. 1977
Shana Devlin
b. 1979
Key
b. born
m. married
d. deceased
- - - adopted
..... illegitimate

CHAPTER ONE

ALEXANDRA RUBBED the sleep from her eyes and stretched awake. Rolling over, she rummaged until her hand brushed across the silky golden hair of her favorite doll. Grabbing her by a worn arm, she pulled the doll against her chest in a comforting hug. Sometimes Mary Jane was afraid of the dark.

"I will not let you do it, Jonathan."

The voice made Alexandra cringe. Her mommy sounded so angry. Something must be terribly wrong.

Throwing her short legs over the bed, she slid to the floor and tiptoed across the room and into the hall. Reaching up, she let her right hand trail along the top of the banister. Mary Jane was in her left hand, her soft floppy legs dragging along the shiny wooden floors.

Alexandra stopped at the landing and peered between the railings. Mommy's red curls bounced as she shook her head hard.

Daddy was mad, too. Really mad. His face was all twisted and he was holding a piece of paper over a candle.

Mommy yelled again just as the grandfather clock started to bong. Alexandra closed her eyes and clapped her palms over her ears to block out the noise, but it didn't help much. One...two...three...four.

The last gong was so loud it sounded as if it were inside her head. Mary Jane slipped from her hand and fell to the floor. When Alexandra opened her eyes again, the living room had turned red. Bright red. Flames were licking at the sofa and climbing the walls.

All she could see was fire and black smoke that hurt her chest and made her cry. She was afraid, so very afraid.

''Daddy, please help me! Daaaadddy!''

''It's okay, Kitten. I have you.''

Safe. In Daddy's arms. But someone was screaming. And screaming. And screaming.

ALEXANDRA JERKED AWAKE as her screams reverberated in the bedroom of her apartment. In frenzied panic, she kicked off the sheet. If she didn't hurry, she would be trapped in the fire.

But when her feet hit the floor, it was the shock of reality that sent her reeling. She cowered against the bedpost, a thin, shivering mass in her nightgown, which was wringing wet with the cold sweat of fear. She dropped back to the side of the bed, bewildered and shaking.

There was no fire. No smoke.

There was only the nightmare. And there was no place to run where it wouldn't follow. She knew. She'd spent the last few years trying. Reality was a thin film over her life, but the nightmare was its very essence. It overrode every decision she made, every emotion she felt—every breath she took.

And it was getting worse every day, the details more defined, the fear more consuming. This time the nightmare had come while she'd slept, but often the fragmented memories attacked even in the bright light of day.

On some level she must have known this would happen if she returned to Seattle, the place where it all began for her—began and ended in a thick, choking blast of fire and smoke. That's why she'd waited twenty years to come back. And why she couldn't stay.

But she couldn't just pick up and run the way she always had before when things got tough—at least not until a few things were settled. The day-care center that she operated with her lifelong friends Hannah and Katherine was yet to be sold. And there was Gary Devlin.

Her heart wrenched at the thought of the dirty, tattered homeless man, who suffered from Alzheimer's and roamed the dark and musty tunnels that formed Seattle's Underground. A lost soul who had come into her life by sheer coincidence? Or her father? She believed the latter with every fiber of her being, and nothing anyone said would convince her differently. Not without proof.

And no matter how bad the nightmares became, she could never leave Seattle until she was certain beyond a shadow of a doubt exactly who Gary Devlin really was.

Shivering, she tugged the wet nightgown away from her clammy body and considered taking a warm bath and then trying to get a little more sleep. After all, it was only six o'clock on a Saturday morning. But if she closed her eyes and tried to sleep, the dream might return. Better to get in a quick jog while the smart, more fortunate people of the city slept, grab a coffee at Caffeine Hy's, then be ready to shower and take on the day's errands.

Some exciting life.

Letting her nightgown fall to the floor, she crossed the room in her altogether and dug a pair of running shorts and a sports top from her closet. Exercise was good for the soul. Her soul could use the help.

HANNAH RICHARDS MCKAY hesitated, the phone feeling heavy in her hand. She'd been hoping for a call from a suitable buyer for the day-care center, but she'd never expected that person to be Dr. Ben Jessup.

"Forrester Square Day Care is for sale, isn't it?" he asked. "Or am I too late?"

"You're not too late."

"Then I'm definitely interested. Would it be possible to meet with you this morning? I know I've seen the place before, but only as a father. I'd like to have another look at it from a prospective buyer's standpoint."

He did sound interested, and prospective buyers were not exactly knocking their door down. Actually, Ben Jessup was the first person who'd shown any serious interest. The problem was that Alexandra would not consider him suitable. He'd gotten upset several months ago, hurled a few accusations of irresponsibility when it came to the children's safety, and yanked his son from their program.

It had all stemmed from the police using the day care for surveillance work. Katherine had really had no choice but to say yes to the police, and as far as she and Hannah were concerned, Ben had groveled sufficiently when he'd subsequently asked them to readmit Doug. But Alexandra had about as much use for the good doctor as she did for a juicy slice of prime rib—which to her vegetarian's mind was practically suicide. Still, she was as eager for the sale to go through as Hannah and Katherine were, so surely she'd cooperate.

"What time would you like to inspect the center?"

"I could easily be there by ten, if that's not too early."

"Ten should be fine, but I'll need to check with my partner Alexandra Webber to make certain she can meet you then."

"I'd rather meet with you."

Yeah. Hannah would like that a whole lot better herself. Unfortunately it wouldn't fly this morning. "I can't possibly make it this weekend, but Alexandra is quite capable of showing you through the day care and answering any questions you have."

"I'm sure she is capable. She can also be as amiable as a pit bull who's missed its last three meals. And that's on her good days."

"Alexandra is outspoken, but she's usually very sociable."

"You can't prove that by me."

And Ben Jessup wasn't all that affable where Alexandra was concerned, either, but no use bringing that up. "The children at the day care love her," Hannah said, hoping to ease his concern, if not her own, "including your son."

"Especially my son. And though I appreciate the way Alexandra's bonded with Doug, that doesn't change the fact that she hasn't forgiven me for my reactions to that police surveillance fiasco. I'm convinced she sees me as an arrogant snob."

So Ben Jessup was not only gorgeous and successful, but perceptive. ‘‘Unfortunately it’s either meet with Alexandra this morning, or meet with me or the two of us sometime next week,’’ Hannah said, offering him an out.

‘‘I’m afraid my schedule’s not that flexible, and I really don’t want to put this off any longer than necessary.’’

In that case Alexandra and the doctor would just have to play together nicely for one day. ‘‘I’ll call Alexandra and ask her to meet you at the day care. If there’s a problem, I’ll get back to you.’’

‘‘Very well. And emphasize that I come in peace, so she can leave her razor-edged tongue at home.’’

‘‘I’ll do that.’’

Once the connection was broken, she dialed her friend’s phone number. There was no answer, which meant she was probably out for her morning jog. Hannah breathed a sigh of relief. She’d leave Alexandra a message to meet a potential buyer at the center and omit mentioning Ben Jessup’s name. That way she wouldn’t protest or just plain refuse to go.

Hannah suspected that some of Alexandra’s resentment of the doctor stemmed from the fact that Ben and his son resided at the same Forrester Square address where Alexandra had lived as a child. Not only was the lot the same, but the house was almost an exact replica of the original.

Hannah understood her friend’s feelings, but Ben was not responsible for Alexandra’s tragic past. And he was the perfect buyer for Forrester Square Day Care, which had been named after the neighborhood in Seattle’s Queen Anne district where all three owners—Katherine, Alexandra and Hannah herself—had lived as children. A successful doctor, Ben Jessup was only in his mid-thirties and already head of pediatrics at Seattle Memorial Hospital. He was also a well-respected leader in the community. And he had funds!

So why in the world was she handing him over to a woman who coiled and hissed like a pit viper any-time the man appeared, when she could meet with him herself?

Her new husband stepped behind her and slipped an arm around her waist. ''Are you ready, sweetheart? Adam and I have the picnic hamper packed and the car loaded. The mountains await.''

Oh, yeah. That was why. Heaven was calling. Dr. Jessup and Alexandra were on their own.

IT WAS FIVE MINUTES before ten when Alexandra turned the corner and started walking up Sandringham Drive to the day care. She actually had five minutes to spare, which was pretty good considering she hadn't noticed the message on her answering machine until after nine. Then she'd had to rush to change into something a little more business-like than the jeans and sneakers she'd planned to wear to Pike Place Market for her weekly supply of fresh vegetables and fruits.

A prospective buyer. The very thought of it seemed to calm her troubled spirit. Katherine was already liv-ing in Alaska with her new husband and instant fam-ily. Hannah was reunited with the love of her life and their wonderful son, and now she was pregnant. Both of her friends had moved on with their lives, and Al-exandra desperately needed to do the same.

A tall, lean man stood in front of the center. He had his back to her, with one arm propped against the door as if he'd rung the bell and was waiting for a response. Early and eager to get started. Good signs, indeed.

Now she was really glad she'd changed into her gray slacks and moss-green cotton sweater. The green of the sweater toned down her red hair a little and matched the color of her eyes. She looked good and she'd be impressive as she expounded on the marvelous programs offered at Forrester Square Day Care—an easy task since the center was a source of pride and joy.

Her optimism fell flat as the man turned towards her and she found herself staring into the face of Dr. Ben Jessup. Surely this was not the potential buyer Hannah had wanted her to meet. But why else would he be standing here on a Saturday morning?

"Good morning, Ms. Webber."

So he wanted to be formal, did he? "Hello, Dr. Jessup."

"It's a beautiful day, isn't it?"

"It's sunny."

"I appreciate you giving up your Saturday morning to meet with me."

"To tell you the truth, I didn't realize you were the one I was meeting." She unlocked the door, pushed it open and walked inside with Ben a step behind.

"Would you have come if you'd known it was me?" he asked as he moved to her side.

"Probably not."

He shrugged his broad shoulders. "At least you're honest."

"It's a family tradition."

"So I've heard. And the Webbers were also known as a very warm, friendly, *forgiving* bunch."

"You made that up."

"Creativity is a Jessup family tradition." He smiled, half mocking, totally intriguing and extremely sexy. The last two facts irritated her. Arrogant men like him should be ugly as the villain in some cheap B-rated horror film. But no, he had to look like the rugged hero in a chick flick.

He was at least a half foot taller than her five-five frame, and wore his sandy-brown hair too long to be stylish. In fact, it was so unruly that he always looked as if he'd been out playing field hockey instead of spending his days in an office peering down kids' red throats.

His tanned skin only added to that impression, and today his clothes did, as well. His jeans were faded and his light blue sport shirt was open at the neck, the sleeves rolled up far enough to reveal a masculine sprinkling of dark hair.

"I say we call a truce for today," Ben said, "and just get down to business. I'd like to start with a tour of the center."

"Why?"

He shot her a puzzled look. "Because I don't make business decisions without full knowledge of what I'm getting into. No shrewd investor does."

Arrogant to the core. She tried to bite her tongue, but failed. "You have an extremely successful practice, Dr. Jessup, one that I'm certain must be very time-consuming. What interest could you possibly have in running a day-care center?"

"I have my reasons."

"I suppose you assume that the only way you can obtain the care you want for your son is to own the facility yourself."

"If I were unhappy with the care Doug was receiving, I'd take him out of the center, not buy it, Ms. Webber."

"Ah, yes. We've been there, haven't we?"

"Can you give me a minute? I need to go back to the car and get my suit of armor."

"I'm sorry," she said, managing an insincere smile. "I really don't have any interest in why you're thinking of buying the center. My only concern is that the children who attend continue to receive excellent care."

He stared at her as if she were some vile bacteria he'd like to annihilate with an injection of antibiotics. "I'd hoped we could conduct this morning's meeting as adults. If that's a problem for you, I'll wait and meet with Hannah."

Drat. She did sound like a sadistic shrew with PMS. Plus, her stomach was screwing into knots, and this guy wasn't worth the discomfort. "There's no problem, and I'm sure the two of us can manage. What would you like to see first, Dr. Jessup?"

"We could start there," he said, motioning to an open door off the central hallway. "And please call me Ben."

"Very well. And you may call me Alexandra."

"The name suits you. A little haughty, somewhat regal."

"I beg your pardon. I am not haughty."

"Then you have me fooled. Now, about that tour."

The man was impossible. Still, she was keenly aware of his nearness as they walked down the hall. Once inside the three-year-olds' room, he sauntered from one play station to the next, stopping at the construction and transportation center.

"One of Doug's favorite areas. He loves those excavators and bulldozers you have in the preschoolers' playroom upstairs," Ben said, stooping to his haunches and pushing one of the metal trucks along the wooden floor. She imagined him doing the same at home with Doug. In a house built on the very spot where she'd once played with her father.

Remnants from last night's terrifying dream crept into her mind. She leaned against the toy shelf, suddenly dizzy and weak.

Ben stood and stared at her. "Are you okay?"

"Of course." But she knew she didn't sound okay and probably didn't look it.

"We can do this later if you don't feel well."

"No." She took a deep breath and forced herself to stand straight. "You're already here. There's no reason not to look around." And hopefully make a fast decision to buy. She wasn't sure she could last a lot longer in Seattle.

BEN KNEW A SMART BUYER should never appear too eager, but by the time they'd examined the building and playground outside, he was firmly convinced that Forrester Square Day Care was exactly what he was looking for. So was Alexandra Webber.

She might hate him, but she was full of ideas. Intelligent, creative, energetic and good with kids. The perfect person to help make the transition from the present owners to him, and to head up a satellite day-care center at the hospital.

But Alexandra had been right on target when she'd said he didn't have time to deal with the day-to-day operations of Forrester Square. He didn't have time to oversee the establishment of the satellite center, either. That's why he needed her. A package deal. He'd buy the center if she'd agree to stay on for at least a year.

The concept was already jelling in his mind. Katherine and Hannah were ready to sell the business and move on because they had new husbands and instant families, but as far as he knew, Alexandra Webber had no such plans. There was probably not a man alive brave enough to take her on. Besides, he'd pay her well and the job would offer new challenges. It would be a win-win situation for both of them.

So why was it he could see Mount Rainier crumbling into gravel before she accepted the offer he had in mind?

"Do you have any other questions?" Alexandra asked. She leaned against the desk in the center's office, her hair disheveled by the breeze they'd encountered when they'd gone out to inspect the playground, her expressive eyes looking almost too bold for her fragile features.

"I'd like to talk more," he said, an idea loosely forming in his mind. "Do you have plans for this afternoon?"

The words hung in the air as if waiting for him to reach out and grab them back. He was tempted to do just that, but if his scheme was to work, he'd have to change her mind about him, and what better way to do that than to take her cruising out to Lopez Island, where he had a vacation cabin.

"I don't mean to be presumptuous," he said, "but I'm sure I'll have more questions as I run over things in my mind, and I promised Doug that we'd take the boat out this afternoon. I hate to disappoint him."

"You shouldn't break promises to children, so I

guess you'll have to ask your questions another day, perhaps on Monday when Hannah returns."

"Or you could come boating with Doug and me. *Doug's Delite* is nothing fancy, but it's a neat little cabin cruiser."

She stared at him for a minute, speechless. That was better than an instant no. "Doug would love having you along," he said, searching for any advantage he could find. "And we could talk. It's a perfect day for it. Sunny. Warm. And not too windy. We could even get in a little fishing if you like."

A look of wistfulness softened her features and, for a second, he thought she might actually accept, but then some stubborn reflex seemed to take over and she shook her head vehemently. "It's out of the question."

"Then you do have plans?"

"I have... There's... It's just out of the question," she stammered.

"In spite of what you think, I'm not an ogre from one of the fairy tales you read to the kids, Alexandra. I won't push you overboard and I definitely won't try to take advantage of you."

"I never thought that you would." She blushed just a little. It surprised him and had a disconcerting effect on his libido. He hadn't been with a woman since his wife's death in any kind of intimate way, and he definitely didn't need any manly urges popping up now.

"It was just a thought," he said, "probably not a very good one."

She stuffed her hands into her pockets and stared at the toes of her loafers. When she finally looked up and met his gaze, her eyes were shadowed, far different from the fire he was used to seeing there. He had the feeling again that something far more monumental than selling the business was claiming her attention today.

"I'm sorry if I upset you."

"It's not you," she said.

"Good." He stood there awkwardly, thinking he should offer help with whatever was bothering her, yet knowing she'd reject his attempt and probably ridicule him in the process. "I appreciate your time," he said, "but I've taken up enough of it. I'll get back to Hannah next week."

She merely nodded and turned away. The room was quiet, with only muted street sounds drifting through the open window to break the strained silence. A dog barking. The blare of someone's horn. A siren in the distance. The siren grew closer, screaming, a fitting accompaniment for the discord he felt, though he knew no reason why he was letting Alexandra's mood affect him.

"I'll let myself out," he said.

She didn't answer. He walked to the door, then turned back. Alexandra's face was ashen, and perspiration dotted her brow. She clasped the edges of the desk, her knuckles white from the pressure.

"You're obviously upset, Alexandra. Is there anything I can do to help?"

She didn't react to his question, didn't seem to even hear him. She was shrinking into herself, as if she'd fallen into a semicomatose state. He crossed the room in two strides and wrapped a supporting arm around her shoulders.

She relaxed against him, and he held her close, his own body traitorously aware of the soft swell of her breasts against his chest. She shuddered as a fire truck passed in front of the center, then seemed to regain a semblance of composure as the siren faded into the Seattle morning.

"I'm sorry," she said, pulling away.

"No need to be sorry, but you're pale and trembling. Have you been ill?"

"No. I'm just a little fatigued. I haven't been sleeping well."

"Then you need to see a doctor, get a full physical, and if nothing else is wrong, he can give you something to help you rest."

"You're right. I will."

"Let me drive you home."

"No. It's not far. I can walk."

"You are one stubborn woman."

"Thank you."

"And I'm a stubborn man who is convinced you shouldn't walk home alone in your condition. So do you ride with me, or do I just hold up traffic and drive along beside you as you walk?"

She stared at him. The fierceness she'd projected earlier had been swallowed up by a vulnerability that made it difficult for him not to want to hold her and to protect her from whatever was eating away at her.

"Okay, Ben. I won't argue. You can drive me home."

The concession pleased him yet made him uneasy. Their relationship had been strained before, but he'd become comfortable with the barbed tension that accompanied their every encounter. He didn't understand this new need to protect her and was certain it would backfire on him.

He'd take her home, make certain she was okay, and then he'd cut out before she looked at him with the same haunted eyes she had a moment ago. Before she forced him to deal with the fact that in spite of all he'd been through since his wife's death, he was still very much a man.

CHAPTER TWO

IT WAS AWKWARD sitting in the car beside Ben Jessup, but Alexandra didn't have a lot of choice. Protesting too much would have just made matters worse, and it was bad enough that he'd had a front-row seat to one of her emotional meltdowns.

She was almost certain he hadn't bought her fatigue story, but she hadn't actually lied. Haunting nightmares and lack of sleep probably did contribute greatly to her inability to handle the muddled memories that attacked with alarming frequency these days.

"It's the three-story house in the middle of the block," she said as they turned onto her street. "The one with the black pickup truck in the driveway and the dark green shutters."

"Nice truck. Is it yours?"

"No. It belongs to the man who owns the house. I rent the studio apartment on the third floor."

"It's convenient that you're close enough to the day-care center you can walk to work."

"It was more necessity than convenience. I don't own a car." She didn't own much else, either, except her clothes, but she was not explaining her nomadic lifestyle to Ben.

He pulled into the driveway behind the truck and opened his door.

"Thanks for the ride, but you certainly don't need to see me to my door."

He glanced at the open windows of her apartment, high above the top of the maple tree in the front yard. "I'd feel better if I didn't leave you to manage the stairs on your own. You were pretty shaky back at the center."

"I'm over the sinking feeling, and I'll be fine," she said, stalking off and leaving him standing by the sidewalk.

He caught up with her before she rounded the house on her way to her private side entrance. The next-door neighbor was outside, following a hairy mixed-breed mutt around with pooper scooper in hand. He waved at Alexandra and gave Ben the once-over.

"Hello, Mr. Brinker."

"Nice day," he called back. "Clearest one we've had in weeks."

Alexandra only nodded and pushed through the wooden door that led to the musty stairwell. Running her hand along the wall, she flicked on the light. No matter how bright the day, the stairwell was always dark. It had bothered her the first time she'd seen the apartment, but the bright airiness of the living area more than made up for it.

"Don't you keep that door locked?" Ben asked.

"I did. The lock broke a couple of weeks ago and Mr. McMillan didn't get around to replacing it before he and his wife left to visit their daughter in Boston. I have locks on the door to my apartment. I'm perfectly safe."

"I can fix the lock if you'd like."

She stopped climbing the stairs, leaned on the banister and looked Ben in the eye. "You know, Ben, you don't have to go to all this effort because you're interested in buying the center. I'm not going to refuse your offer just because I think you're arrogant and a tad obnoxious at times."

"While you, on the other hand, are always charming and friendly."

"Back to the biting sarcasm. I think I like you better this way, with your attitude out in the open."

He exhaled a slow stream of air. "Okay. You're at least partially right. I did have an ulterior motive for asking you to go boating, but the offer to drive you home was based on honest concern."

"So what is this ulterior motive?"

"We can talk about it later."

"There really doesn't have to be a later. Hannah was tied up today, but I'm certain you'll be more comfortable dealing with her in the future."

"You're probably right."

She started walking again. He followed her the last few steps to her door and waited while she unlocked it. When she turned around to thank him and send him on his way, the dimly lit landing was suddenly all Ben Jessup. It wasn't that he was intentionally invading her space, but simply that the landing was narrow and cramped and there was nowhere else for him to be but disturbingly close.

"If you need that medication, don't hesitate to call." He reached into his pocket and pulled out a business card with a phone number hand-printed on the back. "This is my personal cell phone number. I usually answer, but if I don't, leave a message and I'll get back to you soon."

His hand lingered on hers as he pressed the card

into her palm, and the awareness level surged even higher. "Thanks again for the ride," she said, striving to keep her voice even and her tone light. He was offering to help so she owed him a little civility, but nothing more.

"No problem." He turned and took the stairs two at a time and she breathed a sigh of relief. The last thing she needed was some kind of ridiculous attraction to Ben Jessup. Just because he'd shown a trace of kindness didn't mean he wasn't the same arrogant stuffed shirt she'd been dealing with for months.

And even that was probably coming to an end shortly. Whether he bought the day care or not, it would be sold, and her contact with the kids and their parents would cease.

Not that she wouldn't miss the children. She would, especially Doug. Even with Ben Jessup for a father, he was one terrific kid. She stepped into the room, then stopped.

There was a note lying on the floor, as if someone had pushed it under the door. The edges were smudged with dirt. Her heart jumped to her throat and her head grew light as she bent to pick it up.

I need to talk to you.

Just one line. Printed with a shaky hand. No signature. But she knew it was from Gary—from her father. She held the note to her heart. At the very moment she'd been lost in haunting memories, he might have been at her door. And now he'd likely disappeared again into the dark maze of tunnels beneath the streets of Seattle, his mind once again lost in the shadows of Alzheimer's.

Urgency swelled inside her. No matter that she'd always been told that both her mother and father had died that night in the fire, she was convinced that Jonathan Webber was still alive, that he and Gary Devlin were one. In moments of semi-lucidity, her father had been drawn back to Seattle and to her. He needed her to find him and to care for him.

Alexandra started a pot of coffee, then went to the bathroom and splashed her face with cold water. She'd already wasted most of the morning, but she'd still have hours of daylight to search for Gary.

The phone rang as she was draping her good slacks over the hanger. Her heart jumped. Gary had never called her before; but then, he'd never left a note before today, either. Her fingers tightened around the hard metal as she pressed the phone to her ear. "Hello?"

"Hi. I'm glad I caught you at home."

She recognized the voice at once. It was Griffin Frazier. A few months ago the Seattle cop had run Gary's fingerprints through the system and found out his name for her, but he was becoming increasingly reluctant to help her and frustrated by her obsession with the homeless man. Alexandra had dated Griffin for a while, and their relationship had been a bit prickly since she'd told him she just wanted to be friends. Still, she knew he would keep an eye out for Gary. "Have you got any news about Gary?"

"Not for certain, but I got a call this morning from some guy who owns a coffeehouse near Pike Place Market. He thinks he may have seen him last night while he was locking up, but he wasn't certain. Said there was some guy who fit the description I gave him poking around in the trash. He tried to ask the man his name, but when he approached him, the guy took off running then slunk behind some cars and disappeared.''

''Exactly where was this coffeehouse?''

Her hands shook as she scribbled down the address.

''You know, I almost didn't call you.''

''Why?''

''I don't think your chasing around after this homeless guy is safe or sane. It's pretty clear he doesn't want your help.''

''You're wrong, Griffin. He was here today.''

''Here, as in your apartment?''

''Yes. I wasn't home when he came, but he left me a note. He needs to talk to me. I have to find him.''

''That sounds awful fishy to me.''

''That's because you think like a cop.''

''Damn right I do. The FBI warned you to let this go, and so did that agent you hired.''

Alexandra had hired an agency in Texas—Finders Keepers—to help her find out who Gary Devlin really was. Mitch Barnes, a former FBI agent, had been assigned to her case. When the FBI warned her to back off on her search, Mitch had urged her to do as they'd said. Because Alexandra wasn't willing to stop, Mitch had sent his former partner, Ernie Brooks, another retired FBI, to speak to her. Ernie had been in Seattle the night of the fire that had killed her parents. But not even his visit had deterred Alexandra. She was determined to find out the truth.

''I think you should back off.''

''Helping a man who can't help himself isn't illegal,'' she reminded Griff now.

''FBI agents—even retired ones—don't go around

making friendly house calls unless they have a damn good reason for doing it.''

''Then they should have told me their reason.''

''They probably weren't at liberty to do that. This Devlin fellow could have been involved in anything. The Mafia. Assassins. Terrorist activities.''

''He's not doing any of those things now. Most of the time he doesn't even know his own name.''

''Let it go, Alexandra, before you get hurt.''

''I'll think about it.'' She wouldn't, of course, but she didn't want to waste any more time arguing with Griffin.

''How about lunch,'' he asked, ''for old time's sake?''

''I appreciate the invitation, but I can't make it today. I have plans.''

''Yeah sure. But take care, will you? And stay out of those tunnels. They're no place for a woman. No place for anyone.''

''You're right.''

She knew Griffin would see her answer as the evasion it was, but she couldn't help it. She'd return to the underground tunnels today, go down into the dank darkness, the stench. She'd be drawn there as surely as if she were attached to the end of a fishing line and someone were reeling her in.

''Thanks for the help,'' she said. ''And if you hear anything else, keep me posted.''

''Be careful, Alexandra. Be very careful. And call me if you need me.''

''You got it.''

Of course, she wouldn't call for anything except help in finding Gary. Griffin was a nice guy, but he needed more than she could give. That's why she'd ended their relationship. Besides, she had too many ghosts in her bed to make room for a man.

Grabbing her oldest jeans, she wiggled into them quickly. She needed to get on the move. But first she'd change the message on her answering machine to let Hannah know she wouldn't be back until late afternoon. Her cell phone didn't usually work in the tunnels beneath the city, and if Hannah tried to reach her and couldn't, she'd worry, especially with the emotional state she'd been in of late.

But thanks to Gary's note, she knew he was still in the area. Alone. Probably hungry. Maybe sick. And it was breaking her heart to think of him living that way.

Please let me find him today.

LOUIS KINARD sat on the back deck of the home he shared with his wife, Helen, and sipped the strong black coffee he'd grown accustomed to during his years in prison. The world had changed in two decades, or maybe it was just that he'd changed. Grown older, slower, less trusting. Before his conviction, he'd been on the cutting edge. Now he seemed to be standing still, trying to find where he fit into the new order of things. At sixty-two, that was not an easy task.

The back door squeaked open behind him and he turned to see Helen joining him. She'd gained a little weight over the years, but at sixty, with gray showing through her dark hair, she still possessed the same soft sweetness that had attracted him to her the first night they'd met. Love at first sight.

And he still loved her. Loved and needed her, the way he knew she did him. But he had difficulty being the husband she deserved. His life seemed so tangled up with the past. He'd spent twenty years going over every aspect of the crime that had sent him to jail, analyzed every scrap of information he'd been able to come up with, scrutinized the evidence the prosecuting attorney had brought against him. Still he had no closure.

"I thought we might go out to dinner tonight," Helen said, walking to the edge of the deck and pinching dead blooms from a potted geranium. "There's a Thai restaurant near the day-care center. I haven't been there before, but Olivia mentioned that the food was very good."

"Olivia? How did you come to be talking to her about restaurants?"

"She stopped by the day care one day when I was meeting Katherine for lunch. She was full of talk about a new boat she was buying. Actually, I think she wanted her new son-in-law to check it out and make certain she was getting a good deal."

Visiting her daughter when she needed a favor. That was Olivia. Some things never changed.

"We don't have to go out for dinner," Helen said. "It was only a suggestion."

"We can do whatever you like," he assured her.

She shrugged. "What about you, Louis? What would you like?"

"Thai's fine." He knew she wanted more enthusiasm, but he couldn't seem to put on much of a front this afternoon. "Have you heard from Katherine today?" he asked, hoping to get her started talking about their daughter. That was one subject that always lightened her spirits.

"She called a little while ago," Helen answered,

her voice already cheerier. "She barely had time to talk. Little Emily was babbling into the phone, and Kayla spilled her milk. Annie was at a friend's."

"Our Katherine, the little mother. She always wanted a houseful of children. Guess she should have been more careful what she wished for."

"I don't think she'd change a thing," Helen said. "I'm not sure if she's more in love with Nick or with his three daughters."

"I don't guess it matters. They were a package deal."

"Along with a home in the Alaska bush. That's the most surprising thing about all of this. I would have never pictured Katherine leaving Seattle for frozen tundra, and yet every time I talk to her, she's raving about the splendor of the country."

"Love makes everything splendid. It did for us, remember?"

"I remember."

She reached over and fit her hand into his. He took it, held it, and thought of all the times he'd ached for her touch when he was in prison. Sometimes he'd wakened in the middle of night and reached for her, then felt icy cold when he realized where he was and how long it would be before he could hold her while she slept.

"Katherine and Hannah are both in love and happy," she said, "but I worry about Alexandra. Katherine's worried about her, too."

"What's wrong?"

"She's still having those nightmares about the night Jonathan and Carrie died. Actually, it's more than nightmares."

"What do you mean?"

"She's beginning to remember details she's never remembered before, things about the fire and her father. Now she's convinced that homeless guy who's been hanging around the day care is Jonathan."

"Where would she get a crazy idea like that? Doesn't she realize that if Jonathan were alive, he would have moved heaven and earth to be with her?"

"Everyone's tried to reason with her. Apparently she contacted the same agency in Texas that Hannah used to locate her son. The fellow assigned to her case is ex-FBI, and he arranged for his partner, who was in Seattle at the time of the fire, to come up and talk to her."

"Surely he didn't tell her Jonathan was alive."

"It's not so much what he said as the fact that when he started to leave, he called her 'Kitten' and said she should follow her heart."

"Kitten? Jonathan called her that from the day she was born."

"I know. So now she thinks the man was trying to tell her that Gary Devlin and Jonathan Webber are one and the same."

Louis let go of Helen's hand and sipped his coffee, his own mind traveling back through time to that night when all their worlds had collided with destiny. No matter what Alexandra believed, he was certain Jonathan had died in the fire. Louis had been arrested the very next day for embezzlement and selling sensitive aircraft software to hostile Third World countries. Kenneth Richards had been left as the only partner in a business that never recovered. Everything had happened so fast, all without warning.

"Alexandra needs closure," he said. "We all do."

"You most of all, Louis. Prosecuted and imprisoned for a crime you didn't commit. I know you loved Jonathan like a brother, but do you think it's possible he was the one who sold the software into enemy hands?''

''Jonathan? Absolutely not. He would never have betrayed me or the company. I'm certain of that. If he hadn't died in the fire that night, he would have been fighting to prove my innocence. Besides, no amount of money would have made him abandon his Kitten.''

''He had a lot of problems, though I'm sure Alexandra knows nothing of them. He was ready to give up on his marriage to Carrie, and the business was failing. That's enough to make a man do things he'd never do under ordinary circumstances.''

''Not Jonathan,'' he insisted. ''He wasn't that kind.''

''Even good men make mistakes.'' She stood and put a hand on his shoulder.

Her words slid over him, chilling him so that he felt as if a crust of ice had formed around his heart. She'd always trusted him, but there were things she didn't know. He wondered if she'd ever be able to forgive him if she knew the secret he'd carried all these years. He'd definitely never forgiven himself.

''I'm glad that Katherine, Hannah and Alexandra are so close again,'' Helen said.

''Yeah. It's nice to know something good came out of the bonds our three families formed back when times were good.''

''It may never be like that again, but things will improve, Louis. They're already a million times better because you're here with me, but they'll get even better. I know they will.''

Helen had always been an optimist. Lucky that one of them was. He stood, tugged her to her feet and held her close. She felt good in his arms. Really good. The one thing in his world that hadn't changed, though, he realized with a sinking sensation that if the truth ever came out, even Helen might walk away.

Twenty years in prison would be nothing compared to the pain of that.

THE NARROW WALLS were crumbling, the dirt floor littered with threadbare blankets and piles of tattered cardboard. Alexandra knew the materials had been left behind by the homeless transients who'd recently been flushed from the maze of tunnels that ran beneath the day-care center. They hadn't all gone, though. There were some who returned to the same spot no matter how many times they were run off. They came back like salmon returning to spawn, not to the place of their birth, but to a spot where they'd found safety and shelter from the winter rains.

A large gray rat scurried past her feet. She trembled but kept walking, lured from one tunnel to the next by light that crept in through the stained and mildewed beveled glass that covered the openings to the streets above.

Seattle's underground hadn't always been beneath the ground. At one time the buildings had been at street level, but as the dirt roads collapsed into rivers of mud, walkways were continuously being constructed over them, leaving the stores below. When the fire of 1889 destroyed the city, the new streets were built a story and a half above the mire and ruins.

A small portion of the tunnels could be viewed for a fee as part of a profitable tour, which left from Pioneer Square. Other sections were used as basements or underground shops. But the majority of the tunnels were nothing more than a playground for rats and a nesting place for destitute men and sometimes women, who must surely have felt as if they'd been dropped into the bowels of the earth.

She knew Gary had lived here for a while. She'd searched for him here one day—the day she had discovered the doll with the painted smile among his filthy possessions.

Footfalls sounded behind her and she turned to see a hunchbacked man in a pair of dirty coveralls several sizes too big for him. His mouth was dotted with open sores and his skin was so translucent, she felt as if she could see his bones through the thin flesh. He stared at her blankly from squinted eyes, then retreated slowly, walking backward, his shuffling feet raising a choking cloud of dust.

"Wait. I want to talk to you." Her voice echoed, sounding like a raspy plea for help.

He shook his head and clumps of matted hair fell over his forehead. "I ain't bothering nothing."

"I know that. I just want to ask you a couple of questions."

"You one of them religious folks come to save me?"

"No."

"Then what you here for?"

"I'm looking for someone."

"Ain't nobody here but me."

"I can see that, but you may know where he is."

The man averted his gaze, then kicked his worn boot against a half-rotted support post. "Why are you looking for this guy?"

"He knows me. I'd like to help him."

He stared at her for a minute, probably trying to decide if he believed her or not. The homeless had their own set of social rules. They were all fiercely independent, but still they stood together against outsiders.

"What's the man's name?"

"Gary Devlin."

He rubbed his bearded chin with gnarled hands and dirt-encrusted fingernails. "I don't know nobody called that."

"He's frequently confused. He may not know his name. He's about six feet tall, very thin, frail-looking, as if he doesn't get enough to eat."

"That would describe 'bout everybody I know. Mealtime ain't too regular down here, lady. Now, I gotta go."

"No. Please. The man I'm looking for has gray hair and a gray beard. It used to be really long and wild, but it was cut a few months ago."

"Is he that guy that got all cleaned up, then come right back into the tunnels?"

"Yes. That's him. He has a doll with him."

He nodded. "Yeah. He sleeps with that filthy doll—holds it like it was a live baby."

"Then you do know him?"

"I've seen him. He's crazy as they come. Babbles 'bout things don't make no sense."

"Have you seen him lately?"

"I might've."

"When? Where?"

"I don't know where he is now, but a couple of days ago he showed up at the mission to get his food handout. He didn't stick around, though, and I ain't seen a sign of him since."

Disappointment settled inside her, and with it a wave of fatigue. One minute, hope swelled. The next, despair took over. The wild ride drained what little energy she had and left her feeling as if she might collapse at any minute.

The man tugged on his left ear and tilted his head as if he were trying to clear water from it. "Sorry I can't help you."

"You helped. At least I know he's still in the area."

"You got a couple of dollars you can spare?"

She hadn't brought her purse, but she'd stuck some money into her pocket. She was tempted to pull out a ten and give it to him, but she knew the warnings about helping the homeless. Give them food, shelter, warm clothes, but never cash. Too frequently they used it to buy illegal substances on the street, some so tainted they became violently ill.

"I'll buy you coffee and food if you'll meet me above later on."

He shrugged his hunched shoulders. "C'mon, lady. Have a heart. I need a drink. You'd need whiskey, too, if you lived like this."

She needed a drink just visiting here, but they'd both have to do without. She shook her head, turned and started back down the narrow tunnel. It felt more like a tomb now, musky and cool, the road to nowhere. A man was hunched against the wall a few feet ahead of her. All she could see was the back of his head. His hair was thin and wiry, solid gray and poking into his shirt collar.

"Gary."

She hurried towards him, hope surging again. He turned her way. His cheeks were sunken and cadaverous, his eyes almost hidden beneath layers of puffy skin. Her heart tightened. It wasn't Gary, but she felt a wave of pity all the same. There must be a story behind every one of these people.

She moved slowly past the man, her legs heavy, her feet dragging. It was going to be a long, long day.

THE SUN WAS PAINTING the horizon in bands of orange and gold as Ben docked the boat at the Shilshole Marina. The end of a perfect day. Well, almost perfect. The boating had been great and Doug had run and played on the island and even caught a couple of nice fish—with the help of his daddy, of course.

It was perfection the way only Seattle could do it. Bright sun, cool ocean breezes, the snowy peaks of Mount Rainier like giant dollops of whipped cream in the sky. Ben had enjoyed the outing, but it hadn't totally kept troubling thoughts at bay. The day-care center had played all day at the back of his mind, or more to the point, the time and energy it would take to buy and operate it and to get a satellite up and running at the same time.

He was already overworked with his practice and was looking to take on a new partner, if and when he could find the right one. But that might take time. Still, he'd made a promise to his late wife to start up a day care for hospital staff, and he wouldn't rest until he kept it.

The only way this scheme could work was if he had someone experienced and capable, someone like Alexandra Webber, running the whole show for him. But she was as stubborn as she was attractive, and he just couldn't see her agreeing to work with him on this.

Now he wasn't even certain she'd be physically able to handle the task. For a couple of minutes there today she'd looked pale as a ghost—or as if she'd seen one. And when he'd held her…

Damn. That was part of what was bumming him out right now. He hadn't been with a woman since Vicki's death two years ago. It was natural for him to feel something when he'd held Alexandra's trembling body close. Natural, and yet it bothered him all the same.

Bothered him that Alexandra was on his mind at all.

Doug hopped the plastic dinosaur he was playing with across the seat and sat it next to Ben. "Can I watch a movie tonight, Daddy?"

"Not tonight. By the time you have dinner and get your bath, it'll be bedtime."

"Aw. I'm not tired."

"Yeah, but I am."

"Can I take my fish to playschool Monday and show Alexandra?"

"Fish are a little slimy and smelly for show and tell. Why don't we take a picture of it, and you can take that to school."

"Okay."

Alexandra. Great with children. A hell of an administrator. Okay, like it or not, he had to talk to her about his proposal. The worst she could do was say no.

Unless he caught her at a bad time. Then what she might do was anybody's guess.

CHAPTER THREE

BEN WAITED until he'd returned from church services on Sunday morning to place a call to Alexandra, though he'd been thinking of her ever since he'd opened his eyes. That had been at 6:00 a.m., when his human alarm clock had bounded onto the bed with him.

Having Doug in his bed was the best part of Sunday morning, but this time, even while they were tussling and cuddling, it was his promise to Vicki about a day care at the hospital that played on his mind. That and the slim chance he had of getting Alexandra to help him put his plan into action.

Now he listened as the phone rang four times, then Alexandra's voice came on the answering machine.

"Hi. If you're looking for Alexandra Webber, you came to the right place. I'm not in right now, but I'll be home late afternoon. Leave a message and I'll call you back."

Ben hung up. He wanted to talk to Alexandra directly.

"Let's go outside, Daddy. I want to swing."

"How about some lunch first?"

"Peanut butter and jelly sammich."

Ben groaned. "Again?"

"Yes."

"I think we should have squash."

"Yuck."

"Then how about cauliflower?"

"Yuck."

"I know, let's have fried caterpillars."

"Yuck. Yuck. Yuck." Doug half ran, half loped to the kitchen. "Peanut butter and jelly," he sang.

It was the Sunday ritual, a nice one in Ben's mind, especially since he knew Doug got healthy lunches at the day-care center all week long. Sunday morning was for hugs and a little roughhousing, then church, then peanut butter and jelly, outside if the weather permitted.

"You sure are slow today, Daddy."

"Is that right?"

Ben swooped Doug up and set him on the counter beside him while he slapped the creamy peanut butter onto a slice of fresh wheat bread. "You want fast. I'll give you fast."

"You're dripping jelly," Doug said, laughing at the mess Ben made when he switched into overdrive.

Ben grabbed a paper towel and wiped it up.

"Are you going to get a girlfriend, Daddy?"

"Girlfriend? Where did you get an idea like that?"

"From Suzie Jenkins. She wants to be my girlfriend. But she pushes when we're in line."

"I'm not getting a girlfriend."

"Why not? Someone like Alexandra. She doesn't push. And she smells good when she hugs me."

"If I ever do get a girlfriend, I promise she won't push, but it's not going to happen any time soon." Ben poured two glasses of milk, put everything on a tray and started for the back door with Doug bouncing along a step behind. He and Doug were just fine on their own. He didn't need a girlfriend, not even one who smelled nice when she gave hugs.

But he did need Alexandra on his side if he was going to make the satellite center work, which meant he had to call on his best methods of persuasion. Whatever they might be.

DEFEATED. Tired. Hungry. Not the signs of a successful day, Alexandra mused as she trudged through the sunlit streets on the way back to her apartment. She'd returned to the tunnels again, run into three men who'd said they'd seen a man matching Gary's description, doll and all. None of them knew where he was today or where he was sleeping nights. Apparently he was on the move.

A car slowed and stopped in the street beside her. She was aware of it, but didn't look up until she heard a man call her name.

"Ben. What are you doing here?"

"A business matter. Hop in. I'll give you a lift home."

There seemed no logical reason to say no. Besides, she was too weary to back away from the offer of a ride. "I'm probably getting your car all dirty," she said as she climbed into the passenger seat.

"Guess I'll have to take the price of a car wash off my offer for Forrester Square Day Care," he said.

Now, that was news. "You're going to make an offer?"

"I'm thinking seriously about it, if things work out so that I can. Do you have any reservations about selling to me?"

"Not really. You've always been concerned about

Doug receiving the best of care, so I'm certain you'll keep the standards of the day care high."

"I'll do my best. Actually, that's the business matter that brought me your way. I was hoping I'd find you home and we could talk about my plans for the center."

"I can't imagine you drove over without calling first."

"I called. Your message said you'd be home late afternoon. This is very late afternoon. Besides, I thought I might have a better chance at persuading you to talk to me if I appeared in person. I brought steaks."

"I'm a vegetarian."

"Guess I can't wow you with my grilling skills, then, but I make a great salad and pour a mean glass of wine."

"Wowing me won't do any good, Ben. Any offer will have to be approved by Katherine and Hannah, as well, so there's no use wasting time or effort feeding me."

"We have to eat."

"Not together."

He slowed for a car that was backing out of a driveway in front of them and turned to face her. "I'm not asking you for a date, Alexandra. This is strictly business."

"Then why don't we talk at the day-care center during business hours?"

"This is the only time I have available. I wouldn't have this if my neighbor hadn't been available to stay with Doug and get him to bed for me. Tell you what. Forget dinner. Just give me a few minutes to say my piece, then kick me out."

She was being unreasonable, taking her frustration at not finding Gary out on Ben—that and the fact that she couldn't seem to be around the man without becoming defensive and aggressive. But he had driven all the way over, and they did need a buyer for the day care. "Okay, Ben. Dinner and a brief business discussion. That's it."

"So all that talk about easy Seattle women is a lie, huh?"

"Afraid so."

"Bummer."

He smiled, and for the first time she noticed how much Doug favored him. Ben was nice-looking. She'd never denied that. Lots of women would be thrilled to have him at their place for a Sunday evening dinner.

Too bad one of them wasn't getting that chance.

BEN GRILLED HIS STEAK and tossed a green salad while Alexandra showered. It felt strange moving around her kitchen, opening cupboard doors, searching for things that weren't his. Or maybe it was knowing what she was doing a few feet away that was making him a little edgy.

Her apartment was spacious, but short on doors. There was a large living/sleeping area with a Murphy bed she'd left down, and a small kitchen and bathroom, which meant there was only one closed door between them now. And behind that door, she was stripped naked, standing under a stream of hot water while she sponged her body with sweet-smelling soap.

He poured himself a glass of wine and walked to the living room. The decor was simple, a lot of greens and yellows, vivid shades that many locals used to combat the depressing grays that dominated Seattle winters. The furniture mix was eclectic, a variety of prints and woods.

The couch was backed with loose pillows, the kind that invited you to curl up with a good book. Fresh flowers filled a large glass container, and one framed photograph stared at him from the top of a pine bookcase.

He walked over, picked it up and studied the subjects. Three men, three women, three little girls, one boy and a shar-pei puppy, all standing in the sand.

"Did you ever see a happier-looking group?"

He turned. Alexandra was standing in the door to her bathroom, dressed in a pair of shorts that showed off her great legs and a T-shirt that skimmed her breasts, revealing the outline of her nipples. Her hair was clean and shiny, framing her face like wispy feathers. No makeup to hide her shiny nose or cover her soft lips.

"They do look happy," he said, forcing his gaze back to the picture. "Who are they?"

"Jonathan Webber, Louis Kinard, Kenneth Richards and their families."

"The founders of NorPac," he said, recognizing the three men.

"Right, and after the aircraft market hit bottom, the owners of Eagle Aerotech. And the rest is history—or is it news? It's difficult to tell these days, what with so many media sharks in a feeding frenzy."

He didn't have to ask what she meant. Louis Kinard's release from prison the previous fall had started a media blitz. Every newspaper, radio and television station in Seattle reexamined the charges against

Louis—embezzlement and the illegal sale of computer software to turbulent Third World countries. You couldn't really blame the news hounds. The Webbers, Kinards and Richardses had once been as big in Seattle as the Kennedys were in Hyannisport.

Ben sipped his wine. "Where there's a whisper of scandal, there's a Seattle reporter."

"Quickly followed by a hungry pack of them. Actually, we made friends with one, Debbie North."

"Isn't that the reporter who was recently killed in a car wreck?"

"Yes. It was quite a shock. She was so full of life. I still have trouble believing she's dead."

When Alexandra didn't say more, Ben turned his gaze back to the photograph. "This one must be you," he said, tapping his finger on the young girl in the center of the photograph.

"The red mop gives me away, does it?"

"Afraid so." The hair was the same, but the rest of her had filled out quite nicely from the skinny kid with the freckled nose. "Would you like a glass of wine before dinner?" he asked, his voice a little huskier than usual.

"A glass of wine would be great. And then I think we should have that little talk you came for."

"It could wait until after we eat."

"You're stalling, Ben Jessup."

So he was. And backing away from something wasn't his style. "I'll get the wine," he said, keenly aware that his promise to his dead wife rested in the hands of another woman—at least for now.

BEN SAT in an overstuffed chair, worn but comfortable, trying to find some way to say this that wouldn't make Alexandra laugh in his face—or pitch him out on his ear. He waited until she'd had a few sips of the wine, hoping it would relax her and make her receptive.

"It's not just the day-care center I'm interested in," he said, deciding the full truth right up front was the only way to go. "I'd like to purchase the center, then expand to an on-site child-care facility for the children of the doctors and staff at Seattle Memorial Hospital."

"That's pretty ambitious."

"I realize that, but it would fulfill a dire need. As it is, our nurses and staff frequently have trouble finding good child care available at the times they're needed for their shifts."

"It would take a lot of planning to get the satellite up and running."

"I know."

"I can't imagine you have that kind of time."

"I don't. That's why I wanted to have this conversation with you before I went any further with my plans to buy Forrester Square Day Care."

"You don't need our permission to start a satellite. Once you purchase the center, it's your baby. You'll be free to expand as much as you like."

He propped his elbows on his knees and leaned in closer. "It's not your permission I'm looking for, Alexandra. It's your help."

"I don't understand."

"I can't do this on my own. Not only do I not have the time, I don't have any kind of credentials to manage this kind of operation. You do."

"No." She shook her head, the feathered layers

bouncing around her face. "If you're asking what I think you're asking, the answer is a definite no."

"I'll pay you well, and we're not talking about forever. I just need you long enough to make the transition work and to get the satellite up and running."

"That would take at least a year."

"A year that's going to pass anyway. You like the kids. You appear to like working at the center, so what would be so terrible about staying on? The salary is negotiable, but you can pretty much write your own ticket."

"Money isn't the issue."

"Whatever the issue is, I'm sure we can work it out. I know we haven't gotten along too well lately—"

"We haven't gotten along at all," she interrupted. "But even if we were best of friends, I couldn't take your offer." She stood and walked to the window, stared into the darkness for a minute, then perched on the sill and met his gaze. "I'm not the person you need, Ben."

"I think you are."

"That's because you don't really know me."

"I know your work. Don't give me an answer yet. Just think about it. That's all I ask."

"You have a demanding career and a child to care for. That would be more than enough responsibility for most men. Why is buying the center so important to you?"

He sucked in a shaky breath. "Does it matter?"

"I suppose not, but I'd like to know."

And she probably deserved to know, since he was asking her to be part of it. When he thought about it, there was no reason not to tell her. "I made a promise. It's important to me that I keep it."

"You promised someone you'd buy Forrester Square Day Care?"

"Not Forrester Square in particular." He took a minute to get his thoughts together, then plunged in again. "Doug's mother was a doctor, too—an oncologist. She was torn when Doug was born, wanting to spend all her time with him, yet feeling a responsibility to her patients. Every day she wished there'd been a day-care center at the hospital where she could have gone down and breast-fed him, rocked him, held him close whenever she'd had a few spare minutes. And she'd always sympathized with the hospital nurses who had so much difficulty finding good child care when they worked late shifts."

"I can understand those feelings. Really, I can. But I can't help you, Ben. I won't be staying in Seattle much longer." She stood and walked to the kitchen. "We should eat and then you should leave."

The mood between them became even more strained. He'd upset her, and he wasn't even sure why. Before yesterday, he'd thought of Alexandra only as an attractive, independent young woman with a barbed tongue and a lousy disposition.

But she was a lot more complex than that. And in spite of her problems, he was still convinced she'd be perfect to run a child-care center at Seattle Memorial.

Not that it mattered. She'd made up her mind, and he was smart enough to know when he'd hit a brick wall.

ALEXANDRA STOOD at the large windows, her favorite part of her loft apartment, and stared at the night sky.

She was so very, very tired, but sleep would only bring nightmares. The fire. The smoke. The screams.

She went to the kitchen, poured the last of the wine into a clean flute, and took it back to her chair beside the window, the one Ben had sat in when he'd talked of his wife.

Alexandra had to admit that the story had gotten to her. Ben had obviously loved Doug's mother very much and desperately wanted to keep his promise to her. His mistake had been in thinking Alexandra could help him with his project. But he didn't know—and she had no intention of telling him—that the ghosts that lived in her memory were becoming more real than the people who inhabited her world.

If she didn't leave Seattle soon, she'd go completely crazy. Unless... Unless Gary Devlin did turn out to be her father. Then she'd do whatever was best for him.

She leaned back in the chair and closed her eyes. Exhausted, she let her mind drift back into the tunnels as sleep overtook her.

SHE WAS RUNNING, chasing a man who was always a step ahead of her. Her lungs burned and her legs ached, but no matter how she tried, she couldn't catch up with him. Finally she fell against a support post, gasping for breath. Only it wasn't a post. It was a man. She jerked her head up and stared into the face of Dr. Ben Jessup.

Alexandra woke up, her pulse racing. It wasn't the horrible nightmare that usually haunted her sleep, but still she was shaking.

She wished he'd never come over tonight, never talked to her about his dead wife and about the promise he'd made. It wasn't fair for him to pull her into his problems when she had so many of her own.

It wasn't right for him to need her.

ERNIE BROOKS stared at the newspaper article on the back page of the *Seattle Times,* a Sunday edition that he'd picked up at the convenience store. It was about one of their own, a reporter who'd died in a one-car crash. No alcohol or drugs involved. Apparently she'd just fallen asleep at the wheel or somehow lost control of her vehicle and skidded off the road and down a steep embankment. A freak accident.

He'd never met the North woman, but he knew who she was. He'd read her accounts of the scandal that had sent Louis Kinard to prison. She'd been the only reporter to gain in-depth interviews with Katherine, Hannah and Alexandra—the three young women whose lives had changed that night so long ago. He'd played his own part in all of that—a more integral part than he liked to think about.

The newspaper reported the crash as an accident, but just because something looked like an accident didn't mean that it was. He should know. He'd arranged for more than a few seemingly chance events himself during his career with the FBI.

What worried him now was that if Debbie North had been killed for something she'd discovered while investigating the Eagle Aerotech case, then Alexandra Webber's life could be in jeopardy, as well.

He should probably go back to see her or at least make a call. He needed to warn her. But about whom?

CHAPTER FOUR

HANNAH FINISHED READING the brief article and dropped the morning newspaper onto her desk. There was to be a memorial service this week for Debbie North so her many friends and colleagues in the Seattle area could pay tribute to her. It was a nice gesture since her funeral had been back in North Dakota, where Debbie had grown up and where her parents still lived.

The service should bring some closure to the uneasiness Hannah felt about the call Debbie had made to her shortly before she was killed. She told Hannah they had to talk. Now they'd never talk again.

It was tough to lose a friend that way, Hannah thought. She and Debbie had hit it off so well. That was amazing in itself when Hannah considered how much she'd dreaded interaction with any of the other reporters who had dogged them even before Katherine's father had been released from prison.

"You're here bright and early," Alexandra said, swinging into the room.

"I decided to beat the traffic in."

"Liar. You just couldn't wait to hear the report on my meeting with Ben Jessup. That was a very sneaky trick you pulled, partner."

"I know. So how did it go?"

"Could have been worse—I think."

"Then I take it you didn't kill each other."

"Didn't have a weapon on me at the time."

"Is he a good prospect?"

Alexandra frowned. "He's interested in buying the center, but he has conditions."

"Like what?"

"That I'm included in the package to help with the transition."

"Excuse me? Ben Jessup wants you to work for him? That must have been some meeting."

"The first one wasn't, but the second was a real eye-opener."

"The second one! Pull up a chair. I have got to hear this story."

Hannah listened as Alexandra told her of Ben's proposition.

Actually, his promise to his wife did make his wanting to buy the center more reasonable. But Alexandra working with Ben Jessup? She practically bristled every time he came near. The whole idea bordered on ludicrous. But it beat the hell out of her spending all her time in those horrid tunnels.

"What did you tell him?"

"That it was out of the question."

Hannah hesitated, then decided as usual to say what was on her mind. "I think you should consider it."

Her friend scowled. "I couldn't possibly work with that man."

"I doubt you'd see him much. He'd be busy with his practice. It would be a perfect job for you. You're great at organizing and you work well with everyone."

"Everyone except Ben Jessup." Alexandra set her coffee on the corner of the desk, added a sprinkling of artificial sweetener and stirred. "I'm not ready to take on that kind of responsibility."

"So what will you do once the day care is sold?"

"I can't make that decision until I find Gary Devlin."

"But if you find out he isn't your father, you'll have to go on with your life."

"I will, just not in Seattle."

"Oh, Alexandra, I know how hard all this is, but you can't keep running away. This is where you belong. You'll realize that once you get closure on Gary Devlin."

She shook her head. "It's not that easy, Hannah. The fire. The smoke. The screams. They just don't go away."

Desperation clung to her words and Hannah wished there was something she could say that would make a difference. But the past held Alexandra as surely as if she were wrapped in chains.

"I'm sorry to let you down about Ben," Alexandra said. "I know you're eager to sell."

"If Ben really wants to buy, I'm certain we can work something out. I'll offer to help him find someone to manage the operation for him, though I'm certain I won't find anyone as capable as you."

"Good. Now, tell me about your marvelous weekend."

It was a ploy to change the subject, but Hannah couldn't resist the chance to talk about her son or her terrific husband. "My weekend was absolutely glorious. We camped out on Mount Baker. Adam is the smartest nine-year-old I've ever seen. He knows all about bugs. Not that I'm into bugs, but he's such a great kid. We hiked and played like we were explorers."

The wonder of it all hit her again as she talked. Finding Adam and Jack and having them in her life was like all the Christmases in the world wrapped into one. She'd given Adam up for adoption at birth, only to realize nine years later that she couldn't bear not knowing if he was safe and loved.

She'd hired a P.I., and that's how she'd found him. Perfectly happy and living with the last man in the world she would have expected—his biological father, Jack McKay. And in the fall they would have a new baby to add to their happy family.

"How's Jack?" Alexandra asked. "Is the honeymoon still on?"

Hannah blushed, though she seldom did. But the thoughts running around in her mind were so hot, she couldn't help it. "Jack is absolutely, scrumptiously wonderful, and that's all I'm going to say."

"Probably a good idea. You should have some pity on us poor single women who don't have a gorgeous, sexy man to crawl under the covers with."

"You could have had a lot of them, Alexandra Webber, if you ever gave them half a chance."

"Let's not go there."

The front door opened as the teachers began to arrive. The first children weren't expected for another half hour. Alexandra picked up her coffee. "Guess I better get to work. I never seem to get as much done once the kids are all here."

"Me, neither. But first I think I'll call Katherine and tell her that we might have a buyer."

"Tell her hello for me, and that I'll give her a call

later, when I have time for the next chapter in her adventures in the bush.''

Hannah reached for the phone to call Katherine, but it rang before she got the chance. ''Hi, Hannah, what's up?''

''Katherine! I was just about to call you.''

''With good news?''

''Could be.''

''I have good news, too.''

''Don't tell me you're pregnant already?''

''Not that I know of, but I am about to become a mom. The paperwork is ready on Carlos's adoption. I'm flying into Seattle on Wednesday to sign the final forms.''

''Three instant stepdaughters and an adopted son. You are a brave woman.''

''Tell me about it. But it's time. Being a foster mother to Carlos was great, but he's thrilled about becoming a permanent part of the family and wants to be a bush pilot like Nick. Now, what's your news?''

''I think we just might have ourselves a buyer.''

''I like the sound of that. Tell me more.''

''The story starts with a meeting between Alexandra and her arch enemy, Dr. Ben Jessup.'' It didn't take but a minute for Hannah to tell Katherine the little she knew.

''How's Alexandra doing, otherwise?'' Katherine asked once they'd finished talking of the possible sale.

''Drowning in her past. She's talking about leaving Seattle.''

''We can't let her do that, Hannah. She belongs in Seattle. We're her friends and we have to help her.''

"Then we better come up with some ideas fast, before her past completely overtakes her present and runs her right out of town."

WEDNESDAY WAS WARM and sunny, the kind of day Debbie had loved best. It went along with her vibrant personality, her bright clothes and flamboyant ways, Alexandra thought as she filed out of the church with Hannah and Katherine.

"She had a lot of friends," Katherine said, stopping at her car but not getting in. "The service was positive and uplifting, but still I grieve for her, even though I didn't know her for very long."

"And grieving is the last thing Debbie would have wanted," Hannah said. "She would have told us to go and have a drink and toast her bon voyage to whatever adventures await her in the hereafter."

"I think we should do just that," Alexandra agreed. "Let's go somewhere on the water. Debbie always said that sailing on the Sound was the one place she could totally relax."

"I know the perfect spot," Hannah said, "though my toasting beverage of choice is milk these days. We can use my mother's new motor yacht. It's moored at Shilshole Bay Marina, which isn't that far from here. We won't even have to lift anchor."

"We can pick up lunch on the way," Alexandra added, "and eat on deck. Just the three of us. A quiet place to share our memories of Debbie."

"Sounds good to me," Katherine said. "When did Olivia buy a boat?"

"Last month. It's her latest craze. Not that she's given up clothes, men and making money. She just added this one to the list. Actually, I think the new boyfriend had something to do with the purchase. Drake likes boating, so she likes boating—until she loses interest in both of them. It's kind of ironic. She used to give Dad a hard time about all the sailing he did, and now it's one of her passions—as long as Drake Phillips is in her life."

"Your mother does have a knack for enjoying life," Katherine agreed. "But how do we manage to get on this fabulous yacht?"

"No problem. I have a key. Jack checked out the motors and had some repairs done for her. He gave me the key to return for him, but she hasn't stopped by the center to pick it up yet."

"Then it's off to the bay," Alexandra said, "for our own private goodbye ceremony to Debbie."

ALEXANDRA'S USUAL CHOICE would have been a glass of white wine, but today she needed the burn of whiskey sliding down her throat. Whiskey was plentiful in Olivia's well-stocked bar, as were most other alcoholic beverages.

"What do you think Debbie would like most for us to remember about her?" Hannah asked.

"Not her hair. She always hated her hair and didn't have a clue what to do with it." Katherine spread her long legs out on the lounge chair and raked her own shoulder-length chestnut-brown hair away from her face. "I'd say she'd like us to remember her as a top-notch reporter."

"I'll drink to that," Alexandra said.

They all reached over and clinked their glasses.

"Debbie was a dreamer," Katherine said. "That's what I liked best about her. She set her goals and she didn't give up, the same way we did when Hannah and I decided to open Forrester Square Day Care.''

''I liked her smile,'' Alexandra said, ''and the fact that she understood that there were some things about our lives that the public didn't need to know.''

''And her tenacity,'' Katherine added. ''She was certain there was more to the scandal that sent my father to jail, and she was determined to find it. If she hadn't died, she might have eventually uncovered proof to exonerate him. It wouldn't have given back the years he spent in prison, but it would have meant a lot to him.''

Hannah sipped her milk. ''I think she did make an important discovery,'' she said carefully. ''It's only a hunch, but there was something so different about her voice that last night. Excited and yet apprehensive.''

''That would be so sad, and so ironically cruel,'' Katherine said, ''if she had found out something that might finally shed light on the Eagle Aerotech scandal and then died before she could tell anyone about it.''

They talked for a while more about Debbie, about the possibility of Ben Jessup's buying the center, and about their own lives. Finally Katherine stood. ''I hate to go, but it's getting late and I need to do some shopping for the girls and Carlos before I meet Mom and Dad for dinner. Why don't you ride back into town with me, Alexandra? I have to go near your place anyway.''

''Thanks, I'll take that offer, except that you can drop me off at the day care. It's my turn to work late, and I don't want to ask anyone to cover for me. Besides, being with the children will absorb some of the grief.''

''Work if you must, but I think I'll take the rest of

the day off,'' Hannah said. ''It's not often I get to be there when Adam gets home from sports camp, but if I hurry, I'll just make it today.''

''Why don't you join us for dinner tonight, Alexandra?'' Katherine asked. ''Take the heat off me, so I don't have to be the sole entertainment. Dad loves to hear tales of my adventures in Alaska. I wouldn't be surprised if he and Mom come out for a nice, long visit before winter sets in.''

''Sorry, but you're on your own. Once the last kid leaves, I'm heading home for a quiet evening and hopefully a full night's sleep.'' Alexandra stood and gathered the glasses.

''I'm ready to go, and yet I hate to leave,'' Hannah said, languorously stretching to a standing position. ''We have so few times when it's just the three of us together.''

Katherine pulled her pale yellow cardigan tightly around her as the wind picked up. ''Let's make a promise right now that we'll always stay close, and that at least once a year we'll get together, no matter where we are in our lives, no matter where we live.''

They held hands. The three of them on a boat moored on Puget Sound, touched with grief and bound by friendship. Alexandra held on tight, suddenly afraid that the world as they knew it was about to dissolve and things might never be the same again.

''WHAT DID YOU THINK of the yacht?''

''Very luxurious, Mother. But why did you decide on it instead of a small country?''

''You know, Hannah, you're starting to sound like your father. I got a very good deal on the boat.''

''It's nice,'' Hannah said, switching the cell phone

to speaker and shoving the gear into reverse so that she could back out of the marina parking space. "Katherine and Alexandra both wanted me to thank you for letting us use it. That's why I called."

"I just wish you'd had a happier occasion for the visit. I am sorry about Debbie, though I didn't particularly like her or her newspaper stories."

"She was only doing her job," Hannah said, knowing she'd never convince her mother of that and not in a mood to try.

"Digging up a twenty-one-year-old crime serves no purpose. Look how it's upset Alexandra. You said yourself she doesn't want to stay here in Seattle because she can't get over the past."

"She might have if Gary Devlin hadn't popped into her life."

"That homeless man?"

"I told you about him."

"Why on earth is she still trying to connect with him?"

"She wants to help him." Hannah was hesitant to say more, but then again, her mother might be just the one who could help Alexandra. Olivia had been in Seattle the night of the fire and knew firsthand all the details about Jonathan's and Carrie's tragic deaths—if Jonathan had actually died that night. "Alexandra truly believes Gary Devlin could be her father."

"Oh, dear. She is really starting to lose it, isn't she?" Olivia lamented. "The poor darling."

"There are some indications Gary and Jonathan could be the same man."

"No, Hannah. Jonathan is definitely dead. But even if he hadn't died along with Carrie, Alexandra's life would have changed. Jonathan and Carrie were already talking about divorce.''

''I've never heard that.''

''No, and you never will from your father. Not from Louis or Helen, either. They're all so set on preserving the lies and the legends.''

Hannah pulled into the line of traffic on Seaview Avenue. She'd heard her mother's views on the Kinards many times, but this was the first she'd heard that Alexandra's parents had been having marital problems. It must have been a well-kept secret, since it had never come out in any of the media accounts of the scandal. And if that secret had been preserved, there could be others.

''There's no reason for Alexandra to know all of that at this point,'' Olivia said. ''She just needs to call on her faith now and move on with her life. I'm glad you're selling the center. Leaving Seattle might be just what Alexandra needs.''

''She's been running all her adult life. I think it's time she stops. At least here she has friends and roots and people who love her.''

''And hallucinations involving homeless men.''

Hannah sighed. She and her mother had never been on the same wavelength. She didn't know why she still tried. ''Traffic's picking up and I need to disconnect and concentrate on my driving, but thanks again for the use of the boat.''

They said their goodbyes quickly. Now that she was on her way, Hannah couldn't wait to get home. She needed one of Adam's hugs, and one of Jack's, as well. Love was the best healing salve for the sting of death.

But she couldn't shake thoughts of Debbie's last

phone call as she drove home in the afternoon traffic and the glare of a bright Seattle day. Could Debbie have discovered something important concerning the Kinard investigation? And if so, what?

If only the dead could talk, the secrets might have come out years before. Jonathan Webber and Louis had been as close as brothers, and Jonathan would have never let his friend go to prison if he'd known of some way to save him.

Unless their relationship had been a lie, the way Jonathan and Carrie's perfect marriage had been. Sunshine beat down on the car, but Hannah shivered. Something cold and foreign was closing in on her, and she knew that if there was any way possible, she had to find out what Debbie had been so eager to tell her the last night of her life.

THE TRAFFIC was deadlocked, not a car moving as far as Ben could see. It would be the second day this week he was late picking up Doug, and it was only Wednesday. The center made arrangements for parents who arrived late, but he always felt guilty, especially if Doug was the last child left.

He wouldn't have that problem if the hospital had on-site child care. He hadn't given up on it, or on Alexandra. She was hard to figure, but he was still convinced she was the person for the job.

He'd thought about her a lot this week, trying to assimilate the new things he'd learned about her with what he already knew. She had a vulnerable side, one that stirred Ben's protective instincts. And she was feminine. It was evident in the way she moved and the way she'd looked when she was freshly showered, her hair wet and shiny. It was there in the way she'd listened to him talk about Vicki. Truth was, she'd been downright easy to talk to about that.

Finally he pulled into the day-care parking lot. There were no other cars in the lot, which meant Alexandra was likely the one waiting with Doug. An unexpected surge of anticipation shot through Ben and with it a pang of guilt.

There was no reason for the anticipation or the guilt, he reminded himself as he walked to the door. There was nothing between him and Alexandra but business.

His pulse rate just hadn't figured that out yet.

CHAPTER FIVE

THE DOOR AT THE DAY CARE was locked, as it usually was at this hour. Ben rang the bell and waited. When the door opened, Alexandra stared up at him. She was smiling, but her eyes were puffy and red. The protective urge surfaced again.

"Is something wrong?" he asked.

"No. Doug and I were building a garage for his steam shovel. He's finishing it up now."

"You've been crying," he said, then wondered if she'd think he was overstepping the bounds of their dubious friendship.

"I was at a memorial service for Debbie North earlier today. It hit me hard about an hour ago, but I didn't let the children see me in tears. I wouldn't upset Doug."

"No, I didn't mean that. I was concerned about you."

She looked as if she were about to say something then stopped.

The silence was awkward, and it surprised him to realize how much they'd relied on sarcasm to get them through these moments in the past. "Guess it was a really bad day for me to be late," he said, genuinely sympathetic, "but I couldn't have helped it if I'd known. I was admitting a very ill two-year-old to the hospital."

"That takes precedence."

"Is Doug the last one here?"

"Yes. It's not a problem, except that he's been asking for cookies. I told him it was too close to dinner for that, but I was about to call to ask if it was all right to give him some of the spaghetti and green beans we had left from lunch. It's one of his favorite meals here."

"That would have been fine."

"I can still do it. It would only take a few minutes."

"No, we've kept you late enough."

"Daddy!"

Ben looked up. Doug was bounding down the hall as fast as his short legs would carry him. Ben put out his arms and Doug propelled himself into them.

"Come see my garage, Daddy. It's stupendous."

"That's his new word," Alexandra said, smiling. "You'll here it a few dozen times tonight."

"I'm sure." He set Doug back on the floor. "One quick look, and then we have to get out of here and let Alexandra go home."

He wanted to say more, but was hesitant. The peace between them seemed tentative and he didn't want to irritate her by asking if she'd reconsidered his proposal. So he turned and followed Doug, who was already galloping down the hall, eager to show off his construction masterpiece.

ALEXANDRA WALKED OUT the door with Ben and Doug. It was a few minutes before seven, but the sun was still high in the sky. Full dark didn't come before half past ten in July, leaving lots of time for the outdoor activities Seattle citizens were so addicted to.

"Can we give you a ride home?" Ben asked as she locked the door behind them.

"No, thanks."

"I don't mind," he said. "In fact, it would ease my guilt a little for keeping you so late."

"No need to feel guilty. If you'd been on time, I wouldn't have gotten to help make that *stupendous* garage."

"Well, there was that."

Alexandra took a few steps then stopped and squinted into the glare of the sun as a gray-haired man with hunched shoulders walked out from between two cars half a block away then disappeared behind a white minivan.

It was Gary Devlin. She knew it, even though the glimpse had been quick, the distance too great for her to get a good look at his features. "Excuse me," she said, her throat so dry she could barely force the words out. "I have to go." She didn't wait for a reply, but took off jogging, her full skirt twisting between her legs, her sandals skidding along the rough sidewalk.

Her heart was pounding by the time she reached the minivan. She circled it twice. There was no sign of Gary. But he'd been here just seconds ago. Hurriedly she slipped in and out of the street, dodging cars and peering between and around every parked vehicle.

A couple of men in business suits stopped to stare. She shot them a none-of-your-business look and rushed past them. If she let Gary slip away again, it might be days or even weeks before she found him.

The cars were endless, parked on both sides of Sandringham Drive, providing a million places to hide.

Or maybe he wasn't behind a car. He could have slipped between two buildings or be crouched behind some of the shrubbery. "Gary!" She called his name, her pulse racing. Fear gnawed at her insides, the same nameless fear that haunted her dreams, and she felt sweat pooling between her breasts.

"Get into the car, Alexandra."

She spun around. Ben's black BMW had stopped in the street a few feet from where she was standing. "I can't."

He jumped from the car, rushed over and put an arm around her shoulders. "You're shaking and you're pale. Please, just let me drive you home."

She shook herself free of his grasp. "There was a homeless man here a few minutes ago and I have to find him."

"The old man in the gray sweater?"

"You saw him?"

"Yes, but that doesn't mean you can find him now."

"I have to find him," she said. "He needs me." She trembled, feeling the suffocating smoke of the nightmare returning.

"Then I'll help you look for him," Ben offered.

"No. You can't. You have Doug."

But when Ben's strong arms circled her again, she lost the will to resist. She let him lead her to the car. He opened the door for her and she climbed into the front passenger seat.

"I know my behavior seems strange," she said as he shifted gears and pulled into traffic, "but it's really important that I find the man in the gray sweater."

"You don't have to explain. Your reasons for

searching for him are your business. I'll drive slowly and you can look for him.''

She buckled her seat belt, then turned to check on Doug behind her. He was playing with two small plastic dinosaurs, hopping them around his car seat and talking to them as if they were alive. But Alexandra knew he was tired and hungry. He needed his dinner, his bath and his private time with the father he adored.

''Just drive towards Pike Place Market,'' she said. ''If we don't see him there, you can double back and drop me off at my apartment.''

''Will do.''

She leaned forwards, her gaze focused and intense, her mind waiting for the questions that Ben must be dying to ask. To his credit, he didn't say a word. It was as if driving a woman through the streets of Seattle while she searched for a homeless man was as normal as going out for coffee.

It might have been the nicest thing a man had ever done for her. Who'd have ever thought the gesture would come from the infamous Dr. Ben Jessup?

IT WAS ONE OF THOSE perfect evenings when the natural Seattle air-conditioning system went to work at sunset, cooling down the temperatures that had soared during the long summer afternoon. Dinner was finished, the kitchen was back in order, thanks to Jack's help, and Adam was busily engaged in one of his favorite computer games.

Hannah found Jack on the sofa, looking at a fishing magazine. She took it from him and replaced it with herself, snuggling into his arms. Before reuniting with

Jack, she'd thought of love as some intangible quality that fit inside a person's heart.

She didn't think that anymore. Love was hot desire that infiltrated her body at will. It was laughter and touch and sharing her deepest secrets. It was right there in his face, earthshaking, as tangible as strong, sinewy arms and a whisker-roughened chin.

Jack ran the tips of his fingers across her breasts, then tangled them in her hair. "I guess it was pretty rough."

She knew he was talking about the memorial service. "It was difficult and eerily strange," she admitted. "I half expected Debbie to come flouncing into the chapel at any second and laugh at all of us for believing she could be anything but alive."

"Then alive is how you should remember her."

"Hopefully I will someday. For now I can't get past wondering and worrying about why she was so eager to see me the night she was killed."

"She probably just had more questions."

"I don't think so. I've thought about it all day, Jack, and the more I do, the more convinced I am that she'd discovered some new information in the Aerotech case. Something big."

"I guess we'll never know."

"I don't give up that easily."

"So what will you do?"

"I'm thinking I should try to retrace her activities over the last few days of her life. Find out where she went, whom she interviewed, what notes she kept."

"I'm not sure that's such a good idea."

"Why not?"

"The case is over and done with."

"You wouldn't know that by the press we've all been getting lately."

"Even the reporters will tire of it soon. The thing's been chewed into mush."

"But if there's something we don't know..."

"Then maybe it's because Louis never wanted it known." He stroked her hair and kissed the tip of her nose. "Now I think it's time we talked of something more upbeat."

"Like what?"

"Like how terrific you feel in my arms," he whispered.

"You do know how to get a girl's attention." Still, she wasn't quite ready to drop the matter. "But what if Debbie had uncovered something to prove Louis's innocence? It could make all the difference in the world to him."

"Could it? It won't give him back the twenty years he's lost."

"It could clear his name."

"Or it could unleash a whole new scandal that would throw all your lives back in chaos."

"What's that supposed to mean?"

"All I'm saying is that I'd just let this alone if I were you. Let the past and Debbie rest in peace."

It sounded simple enough when Jack said it, but Hannah knew she couldn't do it. Once and for all, she needed the truth.

For herself, for Katherine and especially for Alexandra. It could be painful, one more bitter pill for them all to swallow, but the truth might also be the only thing that could set Alexandra free from the nightmares that were destroying her life.

"So what do you say, my beautiful wife? Are you going to listen to your brilliant and sexy husband?"

"Probably not."

"I didn't think so. So why don't I get us a cup of coffee and you can tell me your strategy for venturing into the world of investigative reporting. And assure me that it's at no risk to yourself."

She smiled as she watched Jack walk away. A wonderful husband. A positively adorable son. And a new baby on the way. She had the perfect life. All she wanted was the same for Alexandra. Besides, there was nothing to worry about. All she was looking for was the truth.

ALEXANDRA FORKED A BITE of cold lettuce, remembering why she never stopped in fast-food burger joints. But when they'd passed this place, Doug had put up a legitimate howl. He was hungry and tired of sitting in his car seat while she peered into the darkness for a man who hadn't materialized.

The establishment was a starvation chamber for a vegetarian, but it was a cholesterol smorgasbord for those into juicy burgers, fries or golden strips of chicken. The chicken was Doug's choice. He'd gobbled it down as if he were starving. Ben had opted for not one, but two loaded burgers. He was on his second now, looking quite contented as he watched his son come zooming down a twisting slide.

Doug ran over to their table, grabbed a sip of milk, then dashed back to disappear once again into a maze of colorful plastic.

"Sorry about the choice of eating establishments," Ben said.

"Prizes and playground. The trappings of any fine restaurant. Do you come here often?"

"About once a month, not necessarily to this particular one, but the same chain. My son is a loyal customer."

"I can tell. He spotted it a block away. Not particularly nourishing, but I suppose there's something to be said for grease and salt."

"An occasional unhealthy meal won't kill him."

"You're the doctor."

"Right. So, now that Doug's squared away, let's tend to you."

"I have my salad."

"I'm more concerned about your general well-being."

"My health is fine. I was tired the other day. It happens to everyone."

"Are you still having trouble sleeping?"

"Sometimes," she admitted.

"Because you're worried about something?"

"Nothing I can't handle, given time." Like a lifetime.

"My guess is that the man you were looking for tonight is tied into it. You were far too apprehensive for that to have been a simple humanitarian attempt to help the homeless."

She felt her insides tightening. "Let's not go there, Ben. It won't help, and you won't enjoy the visit."

"Sometimes talking helps."

"This isn't one of those times or one of those situations."

"You'll never know until you try."

"I have tried," she said.

"Not with me, and I'm a great listener. It's that bedside manner I learned in med school."

She sat, listening to the laughter and chatter of the kids in the nearby play area, hearing the rustle of paper bags being filled with food, the clang of cash registers, the sizzle of frying potatoes. This was real life, no place to slide into horror stories.

Ben wiped his hands on a paper napkin. "I only want to help."

"I know." Everyone wanted to help, but no one could. She met his gaze and the noise and smells of the restaurant faded away. It was the wrong place, the wrong time, the wrong man, and if she told him the truth, he'd doubt her sanity. Yet as unexplainable as it was, she'd never felt such an overwhelming need to pour out all the terror and doubts that taunted her night and day.

"I wouldn't know where to start," she said, hearing the tremor in her own voice.

"In the medical field, we usually begin with what's causing the most pain."

"In that case, you'll get a long story. The pain comes from an old wound, one I received twenty-one years ago in a now infamous fire."

BEN KEPT AN EYE ON DOUG while he listened to Alexandra explain about the nightmare that returned over and over until she hated to even go to bed at night. And always the dreams were of the fire that had burned down the family house on Forrester Square East and taken the lives of both her parents.

"I was lucky to have my mother's family to take me in," she said. "Otherwise I might have ended up being handed over to the authorities and put in foster homes."

"Were they good to you?"

"Wonderful. From the day I arrived at the Cullen ranch in Montana, I was one of the family. My cousin Brad is like a brother, and Aunt Mary Rose and Uncle Walt are two of the dearest people in the world."

"But the fire just never let go of you?"

"I hadn't thought of it just that way, but that's pretty much it. It's like I have to keep reliving that one night of my life. And now there's Gary."

"Your homeless man?"

"Right. The one who walks in and out of my life as if through some invisible swinging door."

"I must be missing something. I don't see how he fits into all of this. Was he a friend of your family?"

"I don't know. Shortly before I moved to Seattle, there was a fire at the day-care center. In the process of putting it out, some homeless people were discovered living in the underground tunnel beneath the center."

"And Gary Devlin was one of those."

"Yes. He hung around the day care after that. I know it sounds strange, but as soon as I started working here, I felt as if he were watching me."

"That must have been frightening."

"You'd think so, but it wasn't. From the very first I had the feeling that I knew him from somewhere."

"Maybe he only reminds you of someone from your past."

"It's more than that. I was working late at the center one night. The others had all left, and I was alone in the office, so engrossed in what I was doing that I didn't hear someone break in. By the time I did, Gary had followed the would-be burglar inside."

"What happened?"

"Gary literally saved my life. But it was more than just his act of bravery that affected me. He picked me up and carried me to safety. And..."

Ben waited. He knew that sharing this was difficult, and he didn't want to push, didn't want to do anything to make this any harder than it already was for Alexandra.

She spread her hands out on the table, then moved them so that their fingertips touched, as if she needed some kind of physical assurance before she could go on. "It was the way he held me, Ben—as if I were a little girl. I felt—like I was in my father's arms again."

"I can see why you want to help him," he said. "You feel a bond with him. It makes sense."

"Not just a bond. There's the doll."

"You haven't mentioned a doll."

She shook her head. "We should go, Ben. It's getting late. You need to get Doug to bed."

"A few minutes more won't matter. Tell me about the doll."

She sucked in a deep breath, exhaled slowly, then leaned in closer. "One day when I was in the underground tunnels looking for Gary, a homeless woman showed me a pile of things that she said belonged to Gary. It was mostly worn, dirty clothes, but there was an old doll in the mix."

"Homeless men probably collect things that remind them of the past, a kind of security blanket."

"This doll was exactly like the one I had when I was young, the doll I lost in the fire."

"Are you sure? That was a long time ago."

"It's the doll in my nightmares—the same painted expression on her face and what's left of the blue-and-white-striped dress on her. I don't remember a lot of my life before the night of the fire, but I remember Mary Jane. God, I loved that doll. I slept with her at night and carried her everywhere I went, as if she were a real baby."

When she looked up at him, her eyes were moist, her composure so fragile it was all he could do not to stand and take her in his arms and just hold her.

"I can't believe I'm telling you all of this."

"You needed to talk."

"I guess."

"So how did you find out his name, anyway?"

"Over the months I befriended Gary—actually, we used to call him Harry. I got him cleaned up and took him for a medical checkup. A friend of mine who's a police officer ran his fingerprints for me."

"Smart move. And I take it that proved he wasn't anyone from your past?"

"The report came back that he was Gary Devlin. He was married to a Charlotte Miles, but had been divorced since 1997. The medical tests showed he's suffering from Alzheimer's."

"Perhaps I can help."

"What could you do?"

"If we can find him, we can take him to the hospital and do a thorough testing. There are drugs that may lessen the symptoms and help him tune in more to his surroundings, though there's no guarantee. And we can start paperwork to have him admitted to a government-sponsored facility where he can be cared for and kept out of the elements."

"I'm sure the government must already know about him, and I don't think they want to help."

"Why do you say that?"

"I hired an agency in Texas that specializes in reuniting family members who've become separated through divorce, adoption, whatever...

"The person assigned to my case was a man named Mitch Barnes, who was formerly FBI. Mitch sent his former partner, a retired agent named Ernie Brooks, to see me since he'd been in Seattle at the time of the fire."

"What kind of information did he have?"

"He was pretty close-mouthed about everything. I asked him to tell me the truth about Gary."

"What did he say?"

"That even if he knew anything, he couldn't tell me. And that I should follow my heart."

"That was it? He told you to follow your heart?"

"Pretty much." She pulled her hands from his, focused her gaze on the play area for a few seconds, then turned back to him. "I don't remember a lot about my father. I only know what he looked like from pictures. But I remember the way he smelled. Like walking in the woods on a fall day. I remember how strong his arms were when he used to swing me up, perch me on his shoulders and carry me down the stairs to breakfast. And I remember him saying 'Good night, Kitten. I love you.'"

"Nice memories."

"Ernie Brooks called me Kitten, Ben."

The last sentence was little more than a whisper. She looked so vulnerable, as fragile as glass.

Doug, with the impeccable timing of a precocious three-year-old, chose that moment to appear at Ben's elbow. He picked up his milk carton, poked the straw into his mouth and slurped the last of the beverage down. "Can I have more milk, Daddy?"

"I think it's time you and your daddy take me home," Alexandra said. "It's getting late for little boys to be out."

"Aw-ww. It's not late, is it, Daddy?"

"I'm afraid it is, Doug. We'll get more milk at home."

"Five more minutes. Pleeease."

"Four and half. And that's final."

Doug dashed off. Alexandra gathered the food containers and napkins and slid them onto the tray. "This will teach you not to tell a woman you're a great listener, Ben Jessup. I'm sure you know more about me than you ever wanted to. Hopefully it's not your duty as a physician to have me admitted to the psychiatric ward of Seattle Memorial."

"Why would I?"

"Some people would claim a sane woman wouldn't believe a homeless man could be her long dead father."

"And former FBI agents don't usually pay visits to people and give them cryptic advice."

"Then you agree that Gary could be my father?"

"Anything's possible. You have to be careful, though. There is a chance that the man you know as Gary Devlin is dangerous."

"He's a lost soul. He doesn't always even know his own name."

"Or else he's a damn good actor. This could all be some sort of scam, or worse."

"If you knew Gary, you wouldn't think that."

"Then I guess I better meet this man. Look, I do

have to take Doug home and get him to bed, but after that I can get Mrs. Harold to come stay with him for a while. She's a widow who lives next door and she treats Doug like one of her grandchildren. I can be back at your place by nine-thirty and we can finish this conversation."

"Most men would be screaming 'beware of the crazy woman' and running away from me at the speed of light at this point, not asking to come to my apartment."

"I'm not most men. Not to mention that screaming and running through a crowded burger joint might be bad for my professional reputation."

"So would hanging out with me. Besides, there's really nothing else to tell. And my health insurance doesn't cover house calls."

She gave him a teasing smile. It looked great on her, though it didn't erase the sadness and apprehension that darkened her eyes. He stood awkwardly, wanting to say more, but having no idea what to say. It had been so long since he'd been with a woman who made him feel this protective—this intrigued. This involved.

It was hard to imagine that until just last week, their every encounter had been caustic. But then they'd never actually talked about anything that mattered to either of them. He'd never watched tears moisten her eyes or seen her tremble from just the thought of the dreaded nightmares.

"You missed the deadline," she said. "It's been five full minutes."

"So the answer's no about my coming over."

"It's no. Talking doesn't change anything. I know what I have to do."

“What is that?”

“Spend time with Gary. See if he has some lucid moments that would give me glimpses into his past. Only…” She stood and stuffed her hands into the pockets of her slacks.

“What is it?”

“Nothing. Let’s just go. I’m tired, and I know you and Doug must be, as well.”

Doug ran between them, grabbed Ben’s hand and tugged on it. “Five more minutes, pleease.”

“Afraid not, buddy.” Doug talked a mile a minute as they walked to the car. Alexandra put on a good front, laughed and teased with Doug the way she always did. Ben didn’t join in. The tale Alexandra had woven was more of a mystery than any novel he’d read in a long time, but it was the woman herself that fascinated him.

Only somewhere deep inside he felt a cold knot of apprehension, as if he’d crossed some kind of line with Alexandra and that there would be no going back.

Or maybe it was just guilt, caused by a sense of loyalty to Vicki.

Whatever it was, he knew he wanted to see her again, and the need was not totally connected to the purchase of the day-care center.

ALEXANDRA OPENED THE DOOR to her apartment and stepped inside, strangely energized by her talk with Ben. He was a smart man and he hadn’t made her feel stupid or as if she were wallowing in foolish hope. Perhaps that’s the reason she’d behaved so out of character tonight, opening up to him and telling him things she'd only shared with Katherine and Hannah.

She had to reevaluate her former opinion of him. He had been headstrong and absolutely wrong about the incident that had led to his taking Doug out of Forrester Square Day Care for a while, but he wasn't as arrogant as she'd chosen to believe.

In the bedroom, she began to slip out of her clothes. She was tired, but dreaded the prospect of falling asleep, only to slip into the terrifying nightmare. The phone rang, a welcome distraction. Dropping her skirt onto the bed, she reached for the receiver. "Hello?"

"Alexandra Webber?"

"Yes." She didn't recognize the gruff male voice. "Who is this?"

"My name's not important. Just think of me as a friend of a friend."

"What do you want?"

"To help you remember the heat and the smoke and the smell of burning flesh. To remind you what it's like to die."

CHAPTER SIX

ALEXANDRA WENT NUMB, her hand frozen to the phone.

"Get out of town, Alexandra, and forget chasing homeless phantoms and digging up the past."

"Is this about my father?"

"Your father is dead. If you stay in town, you'll die the same way he did. The same way your mother did, screaming and begging for someone to save her."

"Who is this?"

But the phone went silent. Alexandra's grip loosened and the receiver fell from her hand and clattered to the table, bouncing against it before crashing to the floor. She gripped the edge of the table, steadying herself.

It was only a phone call. She couldn't give in to the fear, yet already the gong of a clock knelled the deadly hour. Billowing black smoke filled the room. Flames licked their way to the ceiling, consuming everything in sight. Hot as hell. And still she was so very cold. She pressed her hands over her ears to muffle the terrifying sounds of crashing wood and splintering timbers. And the endless, terrifying screams.

"It's okay, Kitten. I have you. You're safe."

But huddled in the middle of the floor, lost in the darkness that had invaded her mind, Alexandra knew that it wasn't okay. The images would subside, but the danger was real. Someone wanted her out of Seattle at any cost—or else they wanted to drive her completely and irreversibly mad.

THE GRANDFATHER CLOCK in the hall began to strike. Ben lay quietly, counting the gongs. Three o'clock. He'd slept some. He wasn't sure how long, but he knew he'd been awake since two. He'd done this nightly for the first few months after Vicki had died. Lain awake for hours on end. Missing her. Wondering how in the world he'd ever be both mother and father to Doug.

But it wasn't Vicki who was on his mind tonight. It was Alexandra of the haunted eyes and terrifying tales of living nightmares. She was still trapped in the past, every bit as much a prisoner as Louis Kinard had been. Only she was innocent, a mere six years old when her world had been taken from her.

But Alexandra wasn't your typical victim. She was an intelligent and spunky woman. There had to be some explanation for why she couldn't get past the night of the fire. Still, whatever secrets lay hidden in her mind had been locked away for twenty-one years. At this point it might take a miracle to figure it all out. A miracle or a very proficient psychiatrist.

His friend would fit that bill. Dr. Jasper Abrams, a foremost expert in the field of dream interpretation as it related to suppressed memories. And he was on staff at Seattle Memorial. Now that Ben thought about it, talking to Jasper was an excellent idea. He wouldn't mention names, wouldn't breech Alexandra's confidence, of course. But if Jasper thought he could help, Ben would definitely talk to Alexandra about seeing him.

Ben crawled out of bed, padded into the hall and made his way down to Doug's room. Easing the door open, he peeked inside. Moonlight filtered through the curtains, dappling the blanket and the delicate features of Doug's face. A lump formed in Ben's throat. There was nothing more reassuring than watching his son sleeping peacefully, his eyes shut tight, his chest rising and falling in gentle rhythm, his stuffed lion nestled in his arms.

After closing the door, Ben tiptoed through the rambling house built to hold the family he and Vicki had wanted, and much too large for just Doug and him. He and Vicki had bought the lot for a fraction of its true worth. No one had been willing to rebuild at Forrester Square East, the spot where Jonathan and Carrie Webber had lost their lives in a terrible fire.

Vicki had held no superstitions or misgivings about the lot. She'd seen pictures of the Webber house and thought it absolutely grand, one of the finest in an area of magnificent historic homes. So when their practices had grown to the point where they could afford to build their dream house, they'd had the architect design a house almost identical to the original.

Until tonight, Ben hadn't given the fire a lot of thought. Now he stopped at the landing and let his gaze travel down the winding staircase, imagining the place in flames and smoke, the way Alexandra must remember it. She'd lost both her parents here, just feet from where he was standing. Doug had lost his mother in this same house. If Ben were the type to believe in curses, he might be wondering now if he'd made the right decision to build on this spot.

But he didn't believe in curses. He believed in science and an occasional miracle. He also believed that men frequently sealed their own fate by the choices they made. Louis Kinard had sealed his. Had Jonathan Webber made a deal with the devil and determined his fate, as well?

What did you really see here that night, Alexandra? What is it that won't let you go?

He walked to the kitchen, pulled a glass from the counter and filled it with cold water. He drank it all as the moon slid behind a cloud, casting the kitchen in darkness. He wondered if Alexandra were thrashing in the nightmare even now. Or perhaps she was looking out her window as the moon's light disappeared. He pictured her in something white with bits of lace. His senses rocked from the image and his body hardened.

Damn. What was wrong with him? If he'd known that being with Alexandra would get to him like this, he'd have never become so involved. She could have just stayed an attractive woman with an attitude. He could be sleeping tonight.

Instead he was haunted by her soulful green eyes and intrigued by her spirit. Worse, he had this crazy need to protect her, though she certainly wasn't asking for his help. If he didn't get a hold of himself, he'd soon be as obsessed with her as she was with Gary Devlin.

And even knowing that, it was all he could do not to pick up the phone and call her, just to see if she was all right.

IT WAS FIVE DAYS after the memorial service for Debbie North when Hannah finally stood in the living room of Debbie's apartment again and stared at the rich wood and the burnt oranges and turquoises of her Southwestern decor. The place smelled of Debbie. Vanilla-scented candles, the faint fragrance of her perfume, and—old coffee.

A half-full cup of the moldy dark brew still sat on the dining room table, as if Debbie had rushed away without taking the time to finish it. The lipstick-stained cup perched atop a pile of notes, enough of them that only glimpses of the wooden tabletop showed through. A stack of old newspapers lay in a pile at the end of the table, next to an open package of Oreo cookies. The scene just as Debbie had left it the night of the accident.

The loss hit again, almost as hard as when Hannah had first gotten the news of the reporter's death, and for a fleeting second she wondered if Jack was right and the whole idea of snooping into Debbie's private life after the fact was a major mistake. But mistake or not, Hannah had to do it. Debbie would not only understand but laud her investigative efforts.

It had taken Hannah days of talking—okay, begging—to get Debbie's landlady to let her in. Actually, even that hadn't worked. She'd finally called Debbie's mother and had her phone Mrs. Perkins to let her know it was okay for Hannah to go through Debbie's things. Now she was taking off an entire Monday afternoon, neglecting her duties at the center to spend her time rummaging through Debbie's apartment.

"This is for you, Debbie," she whispered as she picked up the coffee cup and carried it to the sink. "And for Alexandra, and Katherine's dad, and all the rest of us."

Hannah washed the cup and dumped the stale cookies into the trash before starting to sort through the papers. An hour later she was deep into the stack of notes on the table. The newspaper article she kept going back to had been cut and clipped to Debbie's notebook, portions of it highlighted in neon yellow.

> The fire trucks arrived on the scene at 3:12, within minutes of being called, but the house was already engulfed in flames.

Debbie had made extensive notes about the discrepancy between Alexandra's memory of four gongs and the fact that it was only three o'clock.

As far as Hannah was concerned, the answer was obvious. Alexandra had been only six years old when she'd suffered a tragedy that would have been severely traumatic for any adult. She could easily have confused the number of gongs, especially with her memory of facts so heavily influenced by continuing nightmares.

Hannah skimmed the next few pages of notes. There were notations on virtually everyone who'd been even remotely involved in the Eagle Aerotech crimes, from the Kinards' gardener right up to Paul Marchand, an import-export guy given to smuggling who'd done business with Olivia before his untimely death.

There were also extensive notes about Hannah's mother. That didn't surprise Hannah. Olivia had always generated interest even years ago with her flair for the dramatic and love of being in the social pages. Today, her couture fashion and flawless appearance, along with a steady stream of men in her life and a penchant for making money in her interior design business combined to make her a focus of awe and envy in this city.

Hannah scooted her chair back and picked up an article that had fallen from the table to the floor. More on the Kinard trial. Before she could read it, a light tapping sounded at the door. When she opened it, Mrs. Perkins was standing there, looking like a slightly wilted spring flower in a pair of coral silk slacks and a flowing white blouse. Her long, fake nails and collagen-enhanced lips were painted the same shade of coral as her slacks.

"I thought you'd be gone by now," she said, stepping inside and scanning the room.

"I'm still here," Hannah replied, voicing the obvious.

Mrs. Perkins offered a tentative smile. "I see. How much longer will you be, dear?"

"Most of the afternoon."

"I don't know how you find anything in this clutter. Debbie's parents are sending someone next week to clean out the apartment and sell the furniture to a salvage store."

"What about her personal items?" Hannah asked.

"They had a family member here in Seattle come and remove what they wanted. If there's something you'd like, you can take it. Her parents said to let you have whatever you want. They're very nice, but heartbroken. She was their only daughter, you know."

"Yes, I know."

"I was hoping to lock up now," Mrs. Perkins said. "I'll be away the rest of the afternoon."

"If you'll just leave me a key, I can lock up when

I leave,'' Hannah offered. ''I need to come back tomorrow anyway.''

''Can't you just take what you need today?''

''I can't possibly take all of this.'' She waved her hand to indicate the stacks of newspapers and notes. ''It's much easier to peruse it here.''

''Then I guess I'll have to give you a key. I have a meeting tomorrow, a monthly luncheon with a group of Smith graduates.'' She took the key from her key ring as she talked. ''It's amazing how many of us there are in the Seattle area.''

''My mother's one.''

''Really?'' Mrs. Perkins's eyes lit up and her smile turned genuine, as if they'd just discovered they were closest of kin. ''What year did your mother graduate?''

''I'm not certain,'' Hannah said. ''Mother's fifty-six now, so it's been a while.''

''Amazing. We would have been there at the same time. What's your mother's name?''

''It would have been Olivia Brawney then.''

The landlady put a finger to her chin, as if in serious thought. ''There was a Sara Brawney, from St. Louis. She was a year behind me. Her family was in politics, I think. But I don't recall an Olivia.''

This was the second time that Hannah had asked a Smith graduate from the same year if she knew Olivia Brawney. Both women had answered in the negative. But she wouldn't dwell on that now.

''It doesn't matter,'' Hannah replied, trying to sound convincing.

''Of course it does. We Smith graduates stick together. Why don't you tell your mother to give me a call? She might be interested in joining our luncheon group.''

''I'll do that.'' But Hannah was quite certain Olivia wouldn't be interested in rehashing the past with Mrs. Perkins if indeed they had been at Smith together. Olivia was a woman of action, absorbed in the present and always planning for the future. Now, if there were some rich and influential men involved, it might get her attention.

Hannah went back to the task of organizing Debbie's notes as soon as Mrs. Perkins left. Her gaze caught on one of the larger-type headlines: *Kenneth Richards Questioned In Eagle Aerotech Investigation.*

Her stomach jerked and seemed to turn inside out. She couldn't explain the anxiety when the fact was not news to her. She knew that her father had been questioned. Everyone involved in the company had been interrogated, and the evidence had always pointed to Louis Kinard.

But what if Debbie had found something that had implicated Hannah's father? No. It was a ludicrous thought. Whatever Debbie had found, it could not have possibly implicated Hannah's father in any kind of evil doing. Her mother might have had her indiscretions, but Kenneth Richards was a man of honor. Nothing would ever convince Hannah differently.

KENNETH RICHARDS spread the freshly cleaned sail on the dock to dry. He was happiest these days when he was sailing or working on his boat. Moving into the condo on the waterfront had been one of his best decisions. Another had been divorcing Olivia, though that had actually been more her decision than his.

At fifty-nine, he had life pretty much where he

wanted it. Work four days a week at his consulting job, three days a week to pursue the outdoor life he'd always loved. A life that had been pretty much stress-free since he'd broken up with his last lady friend.

The only people he really needed in his life these days were Hannah and her husband and son. He'd never known Adam existed until a few months ago. But Adam was a gem. And he was going to make a great sailor. One terrific grandchild and another on the way.

Kenneth's cell phone rang. He started to ignore it, then decided it might be Adam or Hannah and ran to get it from the deck chair where he tossed it to keep it from getting wet while he'd cleaned his sails. "Hello?"

"Hi, Dad."

"Hannah, good to hear from you."

"I tried to call you earlier and couldn't get you."

"I was sailing."

"I should have guessed. It's a perfect day for it."

"Not quite enough wind, but I made the most of what there was. Is something wrong? You sound a little upset."

"You know me too well."

"A dad can never know his daughter too well. It's not Adam, is it? He's not sick or anything?"

"No, Grandpa, Adam is fine. I've just had a tough day."

"Children at the day care acting up?"

"I haven't been there yet. I spent the day at Debbie North's, going through her files and notes."

"That sounds a little morbid. I hope you're not still hung up on the fact that she couldn't reach you the night she died."

"Not hung up, just curious as to what she wanted."

"Did you find out?"

"No, but I'm almost sure it had to do with the Aerotech crimes."

He held his breath for long seconds, then released it slowly. "It's ancient history, Hannah. Leave it there."

"I can't—not yet. I know Louis went to prison for selling sensitive software on the black market, but I was never sure exactly what that software entailed? The newspaper articles didn't give much information on it."

"That's because it was considered top secret and classified information at the time. It's not any longer. The software is long outdated."

"What did it do?"

"There were several different types involved, each with separate functions. Basically the programs were used for detection and identification of aircraft. It was state-of-the-art technology back then. Louis had been a key player in its development."

"I think I know the answer to this, but I want to run it by you. If the software was his, why couldn't he sell it to anyone he wanted?"

"We had contracts with the military and the terms of the agreement specified that the software could be sold to no one else. The security of our country was at risk."

"That explains why Louis was given such a long sentence."

"There was nothing wrong with the punishment. They just imprisoned the wrong guy. Louis wasn't capable of such an act, any more than I was, or Jonathan."

"But someone was guilty."

"It's over and done with, Hannah. Let it go."

"Gotta run, Dad. I just wanted to ask about the software. And don't worry, I'm only looking for facts. The truth can't hurt the innocent."

Her words hung in his mind after the call. *The truth can't hurt the innocent.* He was certain she believed that. The young were so sure of the lines that separated and defined right and wrong. He knew better.

There was one truth that might destroy his life—and Hannah's.

THE TIME SPENT at Debbie North's had been a wash, but there was much better news waiting for Hannah when she arrived back at the day care late that afternoon. There was a message from the Realtor who was handling the sale of the business. The woman expected a formal offer from Dr. Jessup any day now.

Her spirits lighter, Hannah went off to find Alexandra to give her the news. The search took a lot longer than she expected. When Hannah finally found her, Alexandra was in the kitchen downing a couple of white pills.

"Are you sick?"

"I have a headache."

"That's because you're not sleeping."

"I sleep some."

But not enough. Alexandra's eyes were puffy and shadowed with dark circles. "I take it the nightmares are still at it."

"You'd think they'd need a night off every now and then, wouldn't you?"

"Have you ever seen a psychiatrist or a counselor about them?"

"A couple of times."

"What happened?"

"I paid out big bucks for them to tell me that I was still dealing with my past. Duh?"

"Then at least see a medical doctor and get something to help you sleep."

"To sleep perchance to dream."

"And there's the rub, but you can't go on like this."

"I'm not. I'm doing everything I can to find Gary. I have to know if he's my father. If it turns out he's not, I'm free to leave town."

"I can't bear to think of you off all by yourself again."

"I know it sounds horrible to you, Hannah. Your whole life is right here in Seattle. But there are just too many bad memories for me."

"You can't keep running."

"Of course I can. I just pack my bags and off I go. That's why I never accumulate stuff. If it doesn't fit in a suitcase, I don't need it."

"Promise me you won't make the decision to leave without at least talking to me and Katherine about it."

"I'll talk, but I can't make promises." She opened the refrigerator and started pulling out cartons of juice for the children who stayed late. "Did you find out anything at Debbie's?"

"No, but I have had a bit of good news since I've been back here. The Realtor called and she thinks Ben Jessup is almost ready to make us an offer on the center. Apparently he's satisfied with my agreement to stay and help him find the right person to manage Forrester Square and the hospital satellite."

Alexandra turned and stared out the window, her

expression grim. It wasn't the reaction Hannah had expected. "You do still want to sell, don't you?"

"Yes. By all means. As quickly as possible."

Hannah watched her friend walk away, fatigue or maybe defeat etched in the slump of her shoulders. It hurt to see her like this. There had to be some way to reach her, some way to help her get past the memories that were killing her as surely as if poison was slowly being released into her body.

The key to change might well lie with Gary Devlin. For good—or for disaster.

When Hannah got back to the office, the phone was ringing. She answered and recognized Ben Jessup's voice on the other end.

"What can I do for you, Ben?"

"I'd like to talk to Alexandra if she's available."

"Sure. Hold on while I get her."

Ben Jessup calling for Alexandra. Hannah would love to know what this was about. Could there possibly be something going on between the two of them?

No way. No possible way.

TIME WAS RUNNING OUT. Ben had to make a decision to buy Forrester Square Day Care or let the matter drop. Hannah had offered her help, but it was Alexandra that Ben wanted and needed. The problem was, his feelings for her were bewildering to the point that he couldn't think straight anymore where she was concerned.

He thought about her at the wrong times. Remembered the wrong things about her. The smell of her perfume. The haunted look in her eyes when she talked of the nightmares. The way she walked. The sound of her laughter.

"Hello?"

"Hi. It's Ben Jessup here."

"Hannah said you'd asked for me."

"Yeah. I was hoping we could talk tonight."

"If this is about buying the day care, Hannah should be in on the conversation, as well."

"It's not that."

"If you only want to talk about my screwed-up life, forget it. Seattle has far more useful projects than me to warrant your attention."

"You underestimate yourself. Have dinner with me tonight, Alexandra."

"Is this about the proposal to work for you once you purchase the day care?"

"I'd still like to have you, but I won't pressure you."

"Then why are you calling, Ben?"

"I've been thinking about the nightmares you have and how they're affecting your health."

"I appreciate your concern, Ben. I really do. But this isn't a medical issue and you're not my doctor."

"All my advice costs is a dinner. I'll even pay."

"I can't make it tonight."

"A hot date?"

"No date, but I'll be hot enough. It's my night for jogging."

"Perfect. I could use a good run myself. How about Alki Beach?"

"Have you ever heard of taking no for an answer?"

"Not unless I absolutely have to." Her resolve was

weakening. He could hear it in her voice. "What time should I pick you up?"

"You know, Ben. I was just beginning to think you might not be as stubborn and as arrogant as I'd originally thought."

"Let's just say I'm persistent when I have a worthy cause. How's eight o'clock? That way I can spend time with Doug and read him his stories before I leave him with Mrs. Harold."

"I'll go, but you're wasting your time."

"Good company. A nice run. A beautiful evening. How can that be wasting time? See you at eight."

Whether it was wasting time or not, there was no denying that he couldn't wait to see her. And that was a very frightening thought.

CHAPTER SEVEN

BEN WATCHED ALEXANDRA stretch, her breasts pressing against the fabric of her stretchy top, her long legs muscled and shapely beneath the nylon running shorts. This new awareness of her amazed him. It was as if even routine movements or smiles affected him.

"You're a pro at this," he said, joining in the stretching routine. "I take it you do it often."

"About three times a week for the past six months," she answered midbend. "It helps clear my mind and makes me so fatigued that sometimes I can actually get some sleep before the nightmares come calling."

"Have you ever run here at the beach?"

"A few times. I like the sights."

"Those bare-chested men playing volleyball?"

"That's not bad, but I was referring to the crowd. There's usually a party or two going on, other joggers, skaters and kids playing at the water's edge."

"And lovers." He pointed to a pair of teenagers perched on the bulkhead who were engaged in some serious face sucking.

"And you can see where that leads," she said, moving over to let a couple pushing a fully loaded double stroller pass. "From kisses to formula."

"You left out a step."

She blushed a little, or else the blood from all the

stretching had settled in her cheeks. Either way, it added to her allure.

"Ready when you are," she said.

"Lead the way."

She took off jogging, slowly, but he was impressed at the easy rhythm of her gait and fascinated by her body in motion. He let her set the pace, somewhat less challenging than his usual speed. But then, he'd been at it since high school. He'd been offered a track scholarship, but he'd turned it down. Even then he'd been dedicated to becoming a doctor and knew his studies wouldn't allow time for the rigorous practice schedule required for meets.

They didn't talk business while they ran. In fact they didn't talk at all, which left him lots of time to think about how he should approach a very delicate matter.

ALEXANDRA GLANCED at her watch. They were right on schedule, back where they'd started in just under an hour. And not a minute too soon. Her lungs burned and her legs were screaming for a break. She slowed, then stopped and collapsed onto a wooden bench near the path.

Ben stopped behind her, his own breathing still steady. "You can go on, Doc, but I've had it."

"I'm just here for the company. You're calling the shots tonight," he said, dropping down beside her. He stretched his legs and raked a lock of thick hair back from his forehead. "You impressed the hell out of me, though. I'd have never taken you for a runner."

She sucked in as much air as her lungs could handle and let her muscles start to relax. Music drifted across the beach, coming from a group of teenagers who had congregated near the bulkhead and were dancing in the sand. Not as couples, just individuals bumping and gyrating to discordant beats.

Alexandra watched them without talking as she took her bottle of drinking water from the holder attached to her belt. She unscrewed the top and held the bottle to her lips, letting the moisture trickle down her throat slowly. She turned to offer some to Ben, but he had his own and was gulping it down, his Adam's apple bobbing as he drank.

Incredibly virile. Disconcertingly sexy. All of a sudden his nearness seemed overwhelming and she took in a ragged breath as she worked to rein in her emotions. There had always been some kind of weird chemistry between them, heated sparks that darted around like crazed lightning bugs. But in the past, the tension had centered around verbal sparring.

She'd love to go back to that. It made things safer. Kept the sizzle manageable.

When he finished drinking, he snaked his arm across the back of the bench. His fingers brushed the back of her neck—just an incidental touch—but her insides quivered a little and she wondered if it had a similar effect on Ben. If so, he gave no indication and his hand stayed on the bench rather than on her shoulder.

"It was a great night for a run," he said. "Cool enough not to melt. I'm glad you suggested it."

"It seemed the only way I could get rid of you," she teased, hoping to keep the moment light. "Now, what is it you wanted to discuss?"

"You don't beat around the bush, do you?"

"Not often."

He tensed a little, then exhaled slowly. "I talked to Dr. Jasper Abrams today. He's a psychiatrist at Seattle Memorial."

"The dream guy."

"Then you've heard of him?"

"There was an article on him in the *Seattle Times* a few weeks ago. Apparently he has a booming practice."

"And a lot of success with patients dealing with repressed memories, especially those relating to recurring dreams. I think you should see him and talk to him about your nightmares."

"I've been there, done that, Ben. I've had shrinks dig around in my mind like it was one of those newly discovered caves in the Cascades. It's never helped."

"It can't hurt to talk to him."

"You're wrong. It does hurt. Besides, I don't have repressed memories. I have ever-present, full-blown recollection of a horrible night from twenty-one years ago."

"Dr. Abrams believes it could be more than that, that you may be fighting the memories because there's something you couldn't face at the time and don't want to face now."

"You talked to him about me? How could you?"

"I didn't mention your name."

"Sure. Like that would make a difference. Everyone in Seattle knows about the fire at the Webber house that left poor Alexandra an orphan."

"We didn't get that specific. I didn't do this to hurt you, Alexandra. I did it because...because I care what happens to you."

And there it was, just tossed into the open and staring her in the face. "I don't want you to care about me, Ben. I don't want anyone to care. I just want people to let me do what I have to do."

"Run?"

"Survive."

"Then do it by fighting to get your life back, not by giving up."

"It's not that easy."

"Nothing that's worthwhile is."

He circled her shoulder with his arm and pulled her close. When she looked up at him, something strange, yet compelling, passed between them, and she knew he was going to kiss her. She should pull away. Instead she leaned in closer.

And then his lips were on hers and she was lost in a need she couldn't begin to understand. The kiss was slow, wet, deliciously ravenous. She didn't want it to end, yet she pulled away.

Ben still held her, but his gaze was directed towards the water. "I didn't mean to do that. It just kind of happened."

"It wasn't totally your fault, but I think we should call it a night."

She expected an argument from him, but to her surprise, he didn't protest. He was no doubt as confused by the change in their relationship as she was, and wary of what he was getting into.

They didn't hold hands or brush shoulders as they walked to the car—didn't touch at all. But the kiss was between them now, pulling them together at the same time it pushed them apart. For good or bad, the relationship had changed forever.

Forever. Even the word was frightening for Alexandra. There had never been a forever for her, and there was little hope there ever would be.

They talked about everyday things as Ben drove back to her place. The traffic. The latest political strife in the mayor's office.

It was dark by the time they pulled in front of her apartment. She opened the door and stepped out. The night air had turned cool or else the heated glow from their kiss had been swallowed by the cold burst of reality. She shivered and wrapped her arms around her chest as she hurried up the walk. She could hear Ben's footsteps, knew he was following close behind her, but she didn't wait for him.

He caught up with her at the side entrance that led to her apartment and followed her up the stairs. When they reached the top, Ben trapped her between his arms and her door. "I'd like to see you again."

"You'll see me tomorrow when you drop Doug off."

"You know that's not what I mean. I'd like to... Look, I'm not good at this. I haven't dated in years."

"And you don't want to start with me. My life is a mess. A hopeless, horrendous mess, and it's not just going to fall into place because I see a new psychiatrist." She turned the key and pushed the door open. "Good night, Ben."

"Don't..."

Without giving him time to say more, she stepped inside then leaned against the closed door, caught up in an ache that seemed to be tearing her apart. She wanted to be normal, to share a kiss, to fall in love. To find the kind of happiness Katherine and Hannah had found, but it was never going to happen.

A biting odor assailed her nostrils. She quickly surveyed the room. Everything was in place—except for a shopping bag sitting in the middle of the coffee table.

She walked over and peeked inside. Candles. Large red ones. Her heart started pounding. She never had candles in the house. Everyone knew that. Her hands shook as she reached inside and pulled out the candles one by one, placing them on the coffee table. At the bottom of the sack was a box of large fireplace matches. And beneath that…

She grew dizzy and sick to her stomach as the odor of gasoline burned her nostrils. Her throat closed. She couldn't swallow, could barely breathe. And finally the scream that had been building inside her since her first peek into the bag escaped. It echoed through the room, but Alexandra didn't hear it.

She was six again, and all she could hear were the terrifying gongs of the grandfather clock, heralding the end of her world.

BEN WAS ALMOST AT the foot of the stairs when he heard Alexandra's scream. His heart slammed against his chest and he raced back upstairs, taking the steps two at a time. When she didn't answer his knock, he turned the knob and pushed, ready to burst the door down if necessary. It wasn't. The door was unlocked.

Alexandra was standing next to the coffee table, bed-sheet white, trembling uncontrollably. He crossed the room in two long strides and took her in his arms. She sank against him and he held her tightly, crooning reassurances in her ear. They stayed that way for a good five minutes, Alexandra cradled in his arms while he tried to piece together what had happened from the visual clues. Candles. Matches. And a gasoline-soaked rag that he'd had to pry from her fingers.

"I don't know why..." Her voice caught on a sob.

"It's okay, Alexandra. Take your time. I'm with you, and I'm not going anywhere."

She nodded and dropped to the sofa. "Thanks." She sat silently for a few seconds, then reached over and picked up the largest of the six candles. "Someone left them for me to find."

"Someone brought you candles?"

"Candles. Matches. And the rag. They were in that bag." She picked up a shopping bag that had been dropped or thrown to the floor and set it beside the candles on the table.

"What jerk would do something like this?" he demanded.

"They didn't leave a gift card."

"Where did you find the bag?"

"On the coffee table, in plain view."

"That should narrow down the possibilities. Who has a key to your apartment?"

"The McMillans. They own the house, but they're out of town. And even if they were here, they wouldn't do this."

"You did lock your apartment when you left, didn't you?"

"Always."

He walked to the door and examined it. "There's no sign of a break-in. Have you had any trouble like this before?"

She took a deep breath, picked up one of the candles and rolled it around in her hands. "I had a phone call the night you came over for steak and salad. It was only a few minutes after you left. I didn't recognize the caller's voice, but he warned me to get out of town, said I should stop searching for a homeless phantom and trying to dig up the past. If I didn't, I'd die the way my parents had, screaming for help.''

Ben searched his mind for possibilities to explain why someone would be so desperate to get her out of town that they'd stoop to this. Gary Devlin? The FBI?

''You should call the police.''

She set the candle back on the table. ''I'll think about it.''

''I don't see what there is to think about. Breaking and entering and threatening your life are serious crimes, Alexandra. And there's no reason to think this won't escalate. Next time you could get hurt.''

''But if I leave town, there won't be a next time.''

''That's no solution.''

''Maybe not the one you'd choose, Ben, but it is a solution.''

Frustration churned inside him, but he didn't want to argue with her when she was this upset. ''Why don't you just sit here and relax and I'll fix you a drink. What would you like? Wine, or something stronger?''

''Hot tea and a shower, but you don't need to stay. I can get both of them on my own.''

''I want to stay. Besides, a gentleman never deserts a woman in distress.''

''In that case, you may have to move in.''

The idea didn't sound half bad. How scary was that?

But things couldn't go on the way they were now. ''Do you have Ernie Brooks's phone number, Alexandra?''

''Yes. Why?''

''I think we should call him. From what you told

me about him, I think he probably knows more than he said. If he does, it's time he talks."

"I don't think he will. The code of the FBI and all that. Besides, it's two hours later in San Antonio than it is here. He's probably in bed."

"Then he can wake up. It's time for some straight talk, and time he and the FBI learn that they're not going to play games with your life."

ERNIE BROOKS WAS ASLEEP in his worn recliner when his phone started ringing. An old rerun of *Hill Street Blues* was blaring away on his TV set, so he lowered the volume and grabbed the receiver, wondering who in the devil was calling this time of night. "Hello?"

"I'm calling for Ernie Brooks."

"You got 'im."

"We haven't met, but I'm Dr. Ben Jessup, a friend of Alexandra Webber's."

Damn. More complications. He wasn't surprised. There had always been too many loose ends in the Aerotech case, and loose ends had a way of turning into loose cannons. "How can I help you?"

"Tell me what you know about Gary Devlin."

"He's a homeless man living in Seattle."

"You know more than that. What's his connection to the FBI?"

"You're talking to the wrong man. I'm retired and have been for years."

"Save the runaround. You wouldn't have come to see Alexandra if you didn't know more than you just admitted. Why is the FBI concerned about her relationship to a transient?"

"Have they contacted her again?"

"No, but someone has. She had a threatening

phone call the other night, ordering her out of town. Tonight someone broke into her apartment and left a little housewarming present for her. Candles, matches and a gasoline-soaked rag."

"Did they leave a note?"

"No. Just the bag of tricks."

"Crazy games played by crazy people."

"This isn't a game, Mr. Brooks. Alexandra's in danger. Is it from Gary Devlin or from someone else?"

"I don't know. And that is the truth. But..."

"Go on, and don't give me any of that stuff about trusting her heart. I need facts."

"I don't have the answers you're looking for. But she should be careful. She should be very, very careful."

Ernie hung up the phone. He'd told as much of the truth as he could, but it wouldn't be enough to let him sleep at night. He'd have to return to Seattle. He'd been the one who'd started this twenty-one years ago. Now he might just have to end it. He and Gary Devlin.

BEN TOOK THE CANDLES out to the trash bin. He'd saved the bag, along with the matches and the rag, and planned to have a cop whose three children were his patients check it over for fingerprints. While Ben was standing there, the man who lived in the house next door pulled into his driveway and got out of a tan SUV.

Ben wiped his hands on his running shorts and walked towards him. "A nice night," he said.

"Yes, it is. Gotta love summers in Washington." He punched the lock button on his magnetic car key and dropped it into his front pocket. "I saw you leaving with Alexandra earlier. Did you two have a nice run?"

"We did. She's a little upset now, though." Ben didn't want to say too much, but if this man had seen them when they'd gone out to run, he might have seen more. "Someone left a shopping bag of trash by Alexandra's door. Did you happen to notice anyone around here tonight carrying a shopping bag?"

"No. I haven't seen anyone hanging around tonight, but then I was out for a while. I watch the McMillans's house pretty closely when they're out of town, though, and I did run off a scraggly looking guy who was hanging around here a couple of days ago. I'll keep an eye open, make sure he doesn't come around again."

"Thanks. If he does, could you give me a call?" Ben handed him one of his business cards. "Call instead of running him off. I'd like to talk to him."

The guy took the card and looked at it before sticking it in his shirt pocket. "Sure thing, Dr. Jessup."

The conversation with Ernie replayed in Ben's mind as he returned to Alexandra's apartment. He didn't see her at first, but he could hear water running in the kitchen. He found her there, rinsing a few dishes. Her hair was still damp from the shower and she was barefoot, the skirt of the short flowered sundress she'd changed into dancing about her thighs.

Desire hit him like a fist to the gut, making it difficult to breathe. This was the time when a smart man turned on his heels and called it a night. And he was nothing if not a smart man. "I guess I should be going, if you're all right."

She turned to face him. Her green eyes were soft

as velvet and totally mesmerizing. ‘‘I know this is a strange request, but could you stay just a little while longer?’’

Stay. He wanted to. He really did. But if he stayed, if he held her again… And yet he couldn’t just walk away and leave her this upset.

‘‘I’ll call and see if it’s all right with Mrs. Harold if I’m out a little later.’’

‘‘Thanks. I’m just not sure I can face being alone just yet.’’

And he wasn’t sure he could face being with her and not touching her, not holding her, not kissing her again. But he could have run from here to Portland easier than he could have walked away from her request.

He realized then that he was falling hard for only the second time in his life. And for the second time, it just might end in heartbreak.

CHAPTER EIGHT

"HELP ME, Daddy. Please help."

Ben jerked awake. He'd fallen asleep in the chair in Alexandra's bedroom. She was still asleep, but she was babbling wildly and fighting her pillow.

He jumped from the chair and rushed to the side of the bed. Easing down beside her, he touched a hand to her shoulder. "It's just a nightmare, Alexandra. I'm right here beside you."

She opened her eyes, but instead of recognizing him or sliding back into reality, she seemed to fall deeper into the hold of the dream. "It's so hot. So very hot, and I can't breathe." She clutched her chest, tearing at the white cotton nightshirt, which was soaked with perspiration.

Ben cradled her in his arms and rocked her to him the same way he did Doug when he woke from bad dreams. "You're okay," he whispered, holding her close. "There's no fire. No danger."

Finally his voice seemed to reach her. She stopped flailing, though her breath still came in quick jagged bursts and her pulse raced.

"Ben?" She said his name tentatively, as if she thought he might be part of the dream.

"It's me, Alexandra. I'm here. You were having a nightmare, but everything's all right."

"The fire. It always seems so real. I feel it, taste it, smell it."

"It was real, but that was a long, long time ago. It can't hurt you now."

"Can't it, Ben? It seems to hurt so much."

"We'll find a way to make these nightmares stop, Alexandra—as long as you don't give up."

He doubted she believed him, but she stayed in his arms and his mind warred with his own needs. All she craved was the safety of his embrace, but it had been two years since he'd been with a woman. He'd expected the old cravings and desires to return one day, but he hadn't been prepared for them to come on him so suddenly—and not with Alexandra.

But his need to protect her was even stronger than his desire, so he held her while the clock ticked away and her body and mind slowly let go of the strain and the fear. It was almost daylight when she finally fell back into a sound sleep.

Gingerly he eased her head onto the pillow. His arms felt painfully empty without her in them, but if he left now, he'd be home in time to shower and dress for work before Doug woke up.

He hoped Mrs. Harold was still sleeping, as well. She was used to him coming home in the wee hours of the morning, but dressed like a doctor who'd been at the hospital tending a critically ill patient, not a jogger.

He tiptoed into the bathroom, took care of business, then splashed his face with cold water. Fully awake now, he thought about the candles and the gasoline-soaked rag. It was difficult to imagine anyone being that cruel, except that he knew it happened. He'd seen enough physically abused children to know that some people were capable of anything.

But this was premeditated, designed to run Alexandra out of town. And whoever had left the package had the key to her apartment. That worried Ben even more than the shopping bag of gifts. She was probably safe now, but she wouldn't be once the person who'd left the candles realized that the scare tactics weren't working. That's why he'd be over tomorrow night to put a security lock on the downstairs door and new and better locks on the door leading directly to her apartment.

He stood over Alexandra's bed for a few moments, watching her sleep. He ached to hold her in his arms again before he left. Instead he walked over to her desk, found a pen and jotted Jasper Abrams's name and number on a pad of paper. He tore the note off and propped it against the alarm clock by her bed so that she couldn't miss seeing it. Whatever was happening now was clearly tied to her past, and it was time Alexandra dealt with it. One way or another, he planned to make certain she did.

It occurred to him as he let himself out the door that he was talking about changing the mind of the most headstrong woman to ever set foot in Seattle.

SMITH COLLEGE, in Northampton, Massachusetts, was a private women's liberal arts college known for its excellence in academics and the accomplishments of its graduates. Hannah scrolled down the page on her computer and searched the college's on-line alumnae directory one last time. Olivia Brawney was nowhere to be found.

Exasperated, she closed the site and logged off the

Internet. She dialed the number she'd jotted down while she was online and let the phone ring. It was early in Seattle, but back in Massachusetts, the business offices of the college would be open. The woman who answered sounded young and eager to help.

Hannah told her she had a résumé of a woman seeking a position at Forrester Square Day Care, and she wanted to ascertain that the records were accurate. She waited impatiently while the woman checked that Olivia Brawney was actually a graduate of the school. By the time the receptionist returned to the phone, Hannah could hear the first group of teachers arriving at the day care.

"I'm sorry, Mrs. McKay, but I don't have any record of an Olivia Brawney having been a student at Smith during the years you mentioned."

"Are you certain?"

"I checked thoroughly. There was one Brawney, but her name wasn't Olivia. Our records show she's married to a state senator from Wisconsin."

"Thanks. I appreciate the time."

"I'm sorry."

"Me, too." Really sorry and totally bewildered, though not surprised. A woman who'd sleep with her husband's friend and business partner would probably have no qualms about lying about her past.

"Hard at work already?"

Hannah looked up as Alexandra stepped into the office, her usual to-go cup of coffee from Caffeine Hy's in hand.

"Have you got a minute?" she asked, and Hannah knew by the strain in her voice that something was dreadfully wrong.

"I have all the time you need. Sit down."

Hannah's blood ran cold as Alexandra described the terrifying gift bag and the phone call from a few nights before. The threats and intimidation were related to the Aerotech crimes. Hannah knew that as surely as she knew that today was Thursday or that her name was Hannah Richards McKay.

"I can't imagine anyone doing something so heartlessly cruel," she said when Alexandra finished the harrowing tale. "But there must be a reason why this person is so desperate to run you out of town."

"Then I wish they'd tell me what it is."

Hannah thought for a minute, debated whether she should say anything, then decided that Alexandra deserved to know. "I think I may be very close to finding out."

"Is this something you discovered in Debbie's notes?"

She nodded. "I've tracked her actions for the last few days before her death. They were all related to the Aerotech case. I think she was on to something when she was killed in that car crash. Something big."

"But the crime was fully investigated years ago."

"Sometimes even obvious facts are overlooked in a case."

"Like what?"

"Debbie made a trip to San Juan Island looking for the antique crystal cross that was stolen from Our Lady of Mercy the night of the fire that killed your parents."

"But the cross was stolen when someone killed Father Michael. That wasn't even related to the Aerotech case."

"Debbie thought it was. She had references to both

cases in her Aerotech notes.'' Labeled with Olivia's name and the date of a garage sale Olivia had held at her vacation house. Hannah wasn't sure why she didn't mention that, except that finding out her mother wasn't a graduate of Smith, as she'd always claimed, had unsettled Hannah more than she'd expected it would. She didn't want to talk about Olivia's possible connection to any of this just yet.

''I've decided to go to San Juan Island on Saturday morning and talk to the people Debbie talked to that day.''

''Maybe you should give this up, Hannah. It's upsetting you. I can hear it in your voice.''

''I can't. This may be important to all of us, Alexandra, especially to you.''

''Then I'm going with you.''

''You don't have to.''

''I want to. We're in this together.''

''Then you're on. Who knows? Investigating might get into our blood the way it did Debbie's, and we'll open our own agency once Ben buys the day-care center.''

''I said we're in this together. I didn't say I was nuts.''

They both laughed, but it didn't do a lot to alter either of their moods.

ALEXANDRA KNEW she had made a big mistake in asking Ben to stay with her last night. The kiss had done enough to entangle them, but when Ben had comforted her after the nightmare she'd let him slip past barriers that no one else ever had.

It had been better when she'd disliked him. She'd been perfectly satisfied and even comfortable thinking him an arrogant jerk with no consideration for anyone but himself and Doug. At least then she'd had a perfectly reasonable explanation for the tension and crackle of emotions whenever she and Ben were together.

Now she had to face the fact that the tension and hyped level of awareness she felt were due solely to his presence. He was a supernice guy, protective and caring. Smart and funny. A great dad. A terrific doctor. And willing to make big sacrifices to keep a promise to his late wife.

All that and still virile, charming and sexy as hell.

It would be so easy to become involved with him. To know he'd be there whenever she needed to laugh or cry. To feel his strong arms around her every day—and every night. To have him kiss her senseless. To make love with him.

The thought danced through her, from her toes to the top of her head, stirring her entire body, awakening a need so strong she grew weak.

No. She had to stop thinking this way. Making love with Ben would be the worst thing she could do. Caring for him would make her start believing that she had a chance at a normal life, that she could find the kind of love and happiness that Katherine and Hannah had found, when Alexandra knew the ghosts from her past would never let that happen.

And letting Ben think there was a chance for them was wrong.

She reached into her pocket and took out the note with Dr. Abrams's phone number printed on it. To Ben, seeing Dr. Abrams was the obvious next step, but she'd taken that step before, with disastrous results. As soon as she'd gone into counseling, the nightmares had intensified.

Fortunately her survival instincts had taken over and she'd packed up and left before she wound up in a straitjacket. She dropped the note in the wastebasket and walked into the events room for morning activities with a small group of preschoolers. She was filling in for the teacher, who had a dental appointment and would be coming in late.

Alexandra was glad for the opportunity. If anything could brighten her spirits, it was the children.

"THAT'S RIGHT, ANN—it's sunny today so we'll put our big sun on the calendar," Alexandra said.

"Who knows what day it is today?"

Half the group put up their hands, including Tommy Atkins, a petite blond boy who always had something to say.

"You can tell us, Tommy."

"It's Thursday, and you know what?"

"It is Thursday. What else do you have to tell us?"

"My mommy's going to have a baby."

"That's great news. I'm certain you'll be a terrific big brother."

"I'm getting a puppy," Alice chimed in. "Puppies are better than babies. They don't wear smelly diapers."

"Puppies are nice," Alexandra agreed, "but babies are nice, too. Does anyone else have any news they'd like to share?"

Five hands shot up, including Doug's. "What's your news, Doug?"

"I'm having a party with ice cream and cake. And we're having ponies to ride. Real ones."

Ponies easily won out over babies and puppies. Doug assured them that they could all come to the party and take a turn on a real live pony. After that, it took a good deal of effort on Alexandra's part to get them back to the task of completing the calendar activities and into the singing games she had planned.

When their teacher arrived to take them back to their playroom, Doug stayed behind. "Will you come to my birthday party, Alexandra? It's nine more days." Doug held up nine fingers so she couldn't get it wrong. "On Saturday."

"It sounds like a great party."

"It's for my birthday 'cause I was sick on my real birthday. I'll be three and a half."

"I'm glad you're getting a make-up party."

"Me, too. We waited until summer 'cause Daddy says July is better for pony rides. I love ponies."

"Ponies are very nice."

"So can you come? Please," he begged, looking up at her with his big brown eyes. She took his hands in hers.

"I wish I could, Doug, but I can't."

"I'll bring you some cake."

"Cake would be very nice."

An invitation to a party at Forrester Square East. In a house that looked so much like the one she'd lived in that she couldn't bear to even drive past it. The same gables and portico. The same dark shutters and white brick. Even the same slate-gray roof.

The memories stole into her mind and chilled her heart. She could all but hear the angry voices of her parents, see her mother's red hair, the curls bouncing as her head bobbed up and down. She could see…

And then it disappeared. She couldn't see anything,

but she could feel the heat, smell the smoke, hear the deafening gong of the grandfather clock. The room begin to spin. Her skin grew clammy. Her legs grew weak.

"Go and get Hannah or one of the other teachers, Doug. Hurry. Just tell them that I need them."

She heard his footsteps as he ran away. Then there was darkness.

"ALEXANDRA. It's me, Hannah. Open your eyes and talk to me, sweetie."

Pulling her mind from the fog, Alexandra opened her eyes and stared at Hannah. It took a second for her to realize that she was lying on the sofa in the office. "How did I get in here?"

"Doug came to get us when you fainted, and a couple of the teachers helped me get you to the office."

"I fainted?"

"I guess that's what happened. You were curled up in a ball on the floor when I got to you, pale as a ghost and muttering things that made no sense. Is this what you meant when you said the nightmares have started coming on you while you're awake?"

"I don't think I've actually passed out before, but this one started the same way. Memories that hit so hard they become my reality."

Hannah took her hand and squeezed it. "What triggered it?"

"Doug Jessup invited me to his birthday party. I started thinking about the house on Forrester Square East, and that was all it took."

"You were calling for Mr. Wiggles. I don't remember anyone named that."

"He was my puppy. The white shar-pei. The dog in the photograph Katherine gave me of our three families together."

"I'd forgotten about him. What do you supposed happened to him?"

"He died in the fire."

Hannah shuddered, feeling her friend's pain and hating that there was so little she could do or say to help. Alexandra had lost her entire world—her mother, her father and her puppy—all in one night, but that wasn't the worst of it. She was still losing them, over and over, day after day, night after night.

"Just lie here for a bit. You need to rest."

"I'm okay now. Once the images recede, they don't usually come back for a while."

"But they will come back. That's why you have to find a way to fight this, Alexandra."

"I've been fighting for years."

"Then you have to keep on trying. If you don't lick this, it's going to destroy you."

"I know." She closed her eyes tight. When she opened them again, they were moist with tears. "I know."

ALEXANDRA GOT OFF the couch as soon as Hannah left the room. She was still shaky and weak, but she hated lying around doing nothing. She'd be better off helping with lunch preparations or pulling weeds in the flower bed out back. Anything beat thinking these days.

Still, Hannah's words seared into her brain as she straightened her slacks and pushed her hair back in place. Now or never. That was pretty much what Hannah had said. Lick it or be destroyed. Easy to say. Impossible to do.

Or was it just easier to shut people out of her life and run away? Run from the past. Run from her friends. Run from life. Run from Ben.

She was already at the door when she stopped, turned around, and went back to the trash basket to retrieve Dr. Abrams's phone number. She'd take it with her, and just maybe she'd find the courage to call him.

THE PAPER with Dr. Abrams's number was still in Alexandra's pocket when she started up the steps to her apartment. Her cell phone rang and she answered it, hoping it was Ben, yet knowing she shouldn't get excited about the possibility of hearing his voice.

"Alexandra, I'm glad I caught you."

"What is it, Griffin?"

"A little news."

"Tell me you've located Gary."

"Not quite, but I do have some information on him. And brace yourself, because you're not going to like this."

"Can we skip the terror tactics and get to the point?"

"Sure. Someone else is combing the area looking for him."

"How do you know that?"

"Some of the homeless guys said there was a brawny guy in a Seattle Seahawk cap asking about him and offering them money to tell him where Gary was sleeping these days."

"Did they?"

"No, but only because they didn't know. You

know how money talks down there. It changes all the rules.''

''Do you think the man who's looking for Gary is from the FBI?''

''It's possible. Or he could be tied to whatever Gary's done that made the FBI warn you to stay away from him.''

''I hope he's not in trouble.''

''If he is, that's all the more reason for you to stay away from him. That's why I called. This is not your typical homeless guy, and every new thing that turns up about him only convinces me more that he could be dangerous. I know I've said this a couple of hundred times before, but you've got to stay away from the man.''

''I'll think about it.''

But not for long. She was nearly at the top of the steps now, and Gary Devlin was standing by her door, shoulders hunched, waiting for her. Gary Devlin and Mary Jane.

CHAPTER NINE

ALEXANDRA STOOD in the hall, staring at the doll and the scraggly, ill-kempt man who held it. She waited until she was standing next to him before she spoke, pushing her words past a choking lump in her throat. "Hi, Gary."

He stared at her, and for once his eyes seemed clear of the glazed confusion that usually dominated his presence. He smiled. "Hi, Kitten."

The pet name sent her heart slamming against her chest. She stared at him, wanting desperately to believe that he was her father, that somehow he'd miraculously survived the fire and was still alive. But caution and the fear that she'd frighten him away made her strive to stay calm.

"It's good to see you again. I'm glad you came."

He stuck out the dirty, weathered hand that held the ragged doll. "This is for you."

Tears wet her eyes as she took it from him. "Where did you get her?"

"I kept her for you."

"Thanks." She put her hand on his, totally sure that he was her father. "Do you remember when I was a little girl? Do you remember carrying me down the stairs on your shoulders?"

But the moment of semi-lucidness had passed. Gary shoved his hands into his pockets and shuffled his worn and scuffed shoes on the carpeted floor. When he looked up, he didn't seem to see her at all.

"Are you hungry?" she asked, still holding the doll.

He nodded.

"Come in, and I'll fix you something to eat."

"I'm all dirty."

"That's okay. I have soap. You can wash."

She unlocked the door and led him inside. Griffin would be furious if he knew she was bringing Gary into her home. But Griffin only knew the cold facts of the situation. He didn't know how Alexandra felt when the older man called her Kitten. How she felt to be standing here now, holding the doll that was so intricately linked to her past.

She took Gary to the bathroom and laid out clean towels for him. While he washed, she threw together as healthy and filling a meal as she could on the few groceries she had on hand. If she'd known he was coming, she'd have bought him the biggest and most expensive steak at the market. Although she didn't eat meat herself, she knew that most men, especially hungry ones, loved a good steak.

She set the table for two, wanting to sit with him while he ate, to soak up his presence and to search for a way to get through to him.

He ate quickly, ignoring her attempts at conversation and barely taking time to chew the half-dozen eggs and four slices of toast. "Do you want more?" she asked when he wiped the last bit of egg from the plate with a scrap of toast.

"I've got to go. I've got to get my bed."

"You don't have to sleep in the underground tunnels," she said. "You can stay here."

He pushed his plate away. "I've got to go, lady. My bed isn't here."

He'd called her "lady." His long-term memory had obviously slipped back into the deep recesses of his mind. "Wait, Jonathan," she said, choosing his real name in the hope it would trigger some fragment of recall.

He didn't even look up. She put her hand on his arm. "I want to show you something."

She hurried to the shelf and took down the framed picture that Katherine had given her. If anything could reach him, it should be the photograph of his family and closest friends. She held it in front of him.

"Look at the picture—this one is you," she said, tapping Jonathan's image with her index finger. "And these were your best friends. Louis Kinard and Kenneth Richards."

He held the picture for a few minutes, then shook his head. "I've got to go, lady. I've got to get my bed."

"No, please. Not yet. Stay and look at the picture. I'll make you a cup of tea." She led him to the couch and indicated that he should sit. The frown didn't leave his face, but he sat down. She put the picture in his lap. "You hold this, and I'll be right back."

Hope was like a fast-acting tonic, making her steps light as she hurried to the kitchen. No matter how impossible it seemed, the man in her living room had to be her father, and he'd kept her doll all these years.

The FBI considered him dangerous, but they were wrong. He was old and sick, his memories locked away and the key lost forever. But he'd sought her out, so there had to be some way to reach him. She wanted him back in her life, no matter why he'd abandoned her and changed his name. No matter what he'd done.

When the tea was ready, she put two cups on a tray with some shortbread cookies she'd forgotten she'd had, and carried them into the living room. But the sofa was empty. And the door was open.

She ran into the hall and looked down the dark stairwell. There was no sign of him, but she raced down the stairs and into the yard. Heart pounding, she searched the area thoroughly, then had to face the truth. Her father had disappeared—again.

Tears escaped and slid down her cheeks as she trudged back to the house and walked up the stairs to her apartment. He was gone for now, but she'd find him again. Hands trembling, she picked up the filthy doll and held it close. Strange, but she could swear she smelled the odors of smoke and burning timbers in the ragged clothes and soft, stuffed body.

"If only you could talk, Mary Jane. The secrets of what happened to Jonathan Webber would all be there in your little lifeless head."

But Mary Jane couldn't talk, and no one else would.

ALEXANDRA PREPARED a salad she had no appetite for, then slipped into comfortable stretch pants and a loose top for her yoga routine. It wouldn't get her visit from her father off her mind, but she hoped it would relax the tightly wound coils her muscles had become.

She dropped to the living room floor and began the slow, deliberate stretches, forcing relaxing images into her mind. A mountain stream, cold to the touch, rushing over rocks and boulders and shooting sprays of water that turned to diamonds when they caught the rays of the sun.

The images shifted. She was sitting on a bench at Alki Beach, feeling Ben's lips touch hers. She stopped midstretch. She couldn't allow herself to fall into this trap. She and Ben had seemed to fit perfectly when he'd kissed her, but that was only an illusion. They didn't fit in the ways that mattered most.

Ben was a respected physician who loved his work. She was a tortured basket case. He had an adorable young son who needed a mother. She'd make a horrible mother. If she didn't stay away from Ben, she would ruin not only his life but Doug's.

The urge to run hit without warning. Instinctively she went to the closet and pulled out her worn luggage. She had to get out of here, go someplace where she didn't know a single soul. Escape Seattle. Escape the memories.

She threw the scarred suitcase to the bed and yanked open the drawer that held her underwear. But Mary Jane sat on top of the bureau, her glassy eyes accusing. Trembling, Alexandra picked her up and collapsed on the side of the bed.

She couldn't leave. Not this time. Not with her father here and needing her. This time she had to stay and face the hell head-on. Still holding the ragged doll, she walked to the table and picked up the paper with Dr. Abrams's phone number. She didn't believe it possible that she could have repressed memories for twenty-one years. Her nightmares were too vivid, too terrifying. If she was going to repress anything, she would have repressed the fire itself.

Yet there were so many questions without answers. And how painful could one visit to Dr. Abrams be?

THE DOCTOR'S OFFICE was on the eighth floor of the medical building attached to Seattle Memorial Hospital by a connecting corridor. Ben's office was in the same building, one floor below.

A nurse entered the waiting room through a side door. "Dr. Abrams will see you now, Ms. Webber. Follow me."

The doctor was at his desk when she stepped inside the treatment room. He introduced himself and motioned for her to sit on a pale blue upholstered chair opposite him. She studied him as she took her seat. He was tall and thin, mid-forties, with a short, well-kept beard, light brown like his hair. He was neither handsome nor ugly, but he did have kind eyes. That had to count for something.

"I know it's difficult talking to a stranger about personal problems, Ms. Webber, but it will go easier if you can relax a bit."

"I'm not sure I can, but I'll try."

"Good." He leaned back in his chair, tented his fingers and smiled. "The patient chart you filled out says you're concerned about nightmares. Do you have them often?"

"Almost every night."

"Are they always the same?"

"Close. There are variations from time to time."

"And how long have you had this recurring nightmare."

"Off and on since I was six years old, but it began to increase in frequency during my adolescence."

"Did it also increase in intensity?"

"Yes."

"And is that still happening?"

She nodded. "The problem's growing worse all the

time. It doesn't always hit at night when I'm sleeping. Sometimes the fragmented memories seem to take over when I'm wide awake, and they're so powerful that I completely lose my focus."

"Do you have some kind of warning that it's about to happen?"

"Very little." She trembled, suddenly inundated by a chill that crept deep into her bones. "It's almost as if the nightmare becomes more real than the present, as if I'm traveling back in time. Sometimes I think I barely make it back to the present, that one day I might not, and that I'll be stuck in that horrible night forever."

"You use the past and the nightmare almost synonymously, Alexandra. Is the nightmare a slice out of your life?"

"It seems to be, though sometimes it takes on new dimensions."

"Why don't you tell me about it?"

"The nightmare or the real past?"

"Whatever you fear the most."

She crossed, then uncrossed her legs, hesitant to loose the nightmare from the dark chambers of her mind. But she was here, and there was no point in paying for a visit if she wasn't going to at least give the doctor a chance to help. She didn't know where to begin, so she started at the place the nightmare usually began. With the loud voices that dragged her out of her bed and into the hallway of the big house on Forrester Square East.

DR. ABRAMS LISTENED carefully, but Alexandra's body language was far more informative than her words. She did indeed travel back in time when she talked of the nightmare. Her reactions were those of a six-year-old. She tangled her finger in her hair and chewed on her lips as she talked of seeing her parents arguing and hearing the gongs of the grandfather clock.

"That's it," she said. "My mother begins to scream, the house goes up in flames, and I wake up." She took a deep breath and finally met his gaze. "And there you have it, Dr. Abrams. Confessions of a woman who's stuck in a nightmare and going nowhere fast."

"You're going somewhere fast, Alexandra. It's just not where you need to be going. I'm sure that's why you're here today."

"I'm here out of desperation." She slipped out of her shoes, tucked her feet and legs beneath her and stared out the window. Her eyes were puffy, with dark circles that she hadn't tried to cover with makeup. No doubt she was near exhaustion, losing sleep night after night. And exhaustion could do strange things to mind control; make a person imagine all sorts of terrors that didn't exist. He'd seen it happen in countless patients.

"What do you think will help, Alexandra?"

"Nothing. I don't think anything will help."

"I disagree. I think there's a good chance you can regain your life—if you're willing to work with me."

She ran her hands along the strap of her handbag, then uncurled her legs and poked her stockinged feet back in her shoes. Ready to run away. But she wasn't a coward. If she were, this kind of persistent nightmare would have finished her off long ago. She was a fighter, but even he feared what she was up against.

"I don't doubt your skill, Dr. Abrams, but you

should know that I've been in counseling before. It only made things worse."

She sounded as if she were ready to give up, but Jasper knew that if she were, she wouldn't be sitting here today. And he doubted he'd ever had a patient who needed closure more than this spunky redhead with the haunted green eyes.

"Have you ever tried hypnosis, Alexandra?"

She wrapped her arms around her chest, as if she'd felt a sudden icy blast. "No," she answered, "and I wouldn't want to."

"Not even if it would end the nightmares?"

"I don't see how it could."

"Hypnosis can be very effective in helping people uncover facts or misconceptions hidden away so deep in their subconscious that they can't reach them on their own."

"I have too many memories, Dr. Abrams, not too few."

"But you may not have the right ones. Perhaps they were too horrible for you to face at six. Maybe you're still afraid to face them."

"I lost both my parents. What could be more horrifying than that?"

"I don't know, but we could find out. But there is some risk involved."

"What kind of risk?"

"The truth you discover may be more destructive than the nightmares, though in your case, I find that hard to believe."

She trembled, then stood and faced him across the desk. "I'll have to think about it."

"I understand. Either way, I'd like to see you again."

She nodded, so ready to bolt, he was surprised she wasn't running to the door. He couldn't imagine what might be locked away inside her mind, but he did know if she didn't face it soon, it would destroy her.

It might destroy her even if she did.

ALEXANDRA BARELY NOTICED where she was walking as she rushed through the waiting room and pushed through the door and into the hall. It had been difficult talking with Dr. Abrams, and she'd had to hold tight to her emotions every second to keep them in check, to keep from sliding into the abyss of the nightmare.

But there was no way she could do that if she were hypnotized. She'd be in the fire. She'd hear her mother's screams. She might even smell burning flesh. Shaking, Alexandra leaned against the wall as a tear escaped and slid down her cheek.

Someone touched her arm. She looked up and saw Ben. The next thing she knew she was in his arms and holding on to him as if he were the only thing between her and the pits of hell.

CHAPTER TEN

ALEXANDRA HAD FOLLOWED Ben's lead almost blindly, paying little attention to where they were going until they reached a door marked Dr. Ben Jessup, Pediatrician. She balked and pulled away from him. "I can't go in there, Ben. I don't want your patients and staff to see me this upset."

"There's no one to see you. They've all gone for the day." He pulled a key ring from his pocket, inserted a key and unlocked the door. "It will be quiet here. We can talk."

"There's nothing to talk about. Besides, you need to pick up Doug."

"I called Mrs. Harold when you told me you'd made the appointment for five. She's picking up Doug today."

"Why did you do that?"

"I thought you might need some company after the session. I knew you were nervous about going."

He tugged her inside. "We'll be more comfortable in my office," he said, leading her through the waiting room and down a narrow hall. She knew she shouldn't stay, but she was drained from the session with Dr. Abrams and didn't have the strength to fight Ben or her need to be with him.

"Sit here," he said, leading her to a sofa that

hugged the back wall. "Can I get you something to drink? Water? Or a soda?"

"Water would be nice."

"Okay. You just stay put. I'll be right back." She watched him walk away, his white coat swinging around his hips. He always looked a little bigger than life and oozing assurance, but here, in the center of his professional world, that confidence was even more evident.

When he returned with the water, he handed it to her, then joined her on the sofa. "You seem awfully shaken. I hope that means you had some kind of breakthrough."

"No."

"But the session went okay?"

"It went as I expected. I told Dr. Abrams about my past and the recurring nightmare. He asked questions and nodded his head. That's what psychiatrists do. They think if they push the right buttons, the patients can reach inside themselves and find solutions to everything."

"Did you reach inside yourself?"

"I've been reaching for years. There are no answers, Ben."

"There are answers somewhere, and we'll find them."

She told him the doctor had suggested hypnosis, and wasn't surprised when he was excited about the possibility. He saw it as a quick fix. She saw it as another dead end, one with the power to drag her deeper into the terror that was driving her mad.

He pulled her close. It would be nice to stay this way, cuddled in his arms, believing, as he did, that all they had to do was want this badly enough and it would happen. But it just wasn't so.

"I really do have to go, Ben."

"Why? Did I do or say something wrong?"

"No, you've done and said everything right. You always do. That's the problem. If I stay, we'll become more involved, emotionally and physically."

"Would that be so terrible?"

"You are not making this easy."

"I'm not trying to make your leaving easy. I want to be with you. I want to spend time with you. I want you in my life."

"I have nothing to offer. Look around you. You have it all. And I'm falling apart faster than a tower of blocks in a roomful of two-year-olds."

"You can lick this thing, Alexandra. Dr. Abrams will help, and so will I and all your friends."

"The odds are against me."

"Damn the odds."

He kissed her, softly at first, but the kiss deepened quickly. Desire swelled inside her. She ached for his touch and his kiss, but if she stayed... She jerked away. "I can't do this."

He exhaled sharply, then moved from the sofa to the chair behind his desk. "Explain the game plan to me, Alexandra. I care for you—a lot. You couldn't kiss that way if you didn't feel something for me. So how long do we have to keep fighting to stay apart when we both want to be together?"

"It's not a game, Ben. This is as much for you as for me. I have too many problems to get involved with you."

"So, if I play by your rules and promise not to

touch you or kiss you or have any other intimate contact, when can I see you again?"

"I'll have to think about that."

"Then let me help you think. What about Saturday? Doug's spending the day with a friend. We can take the boat out if the weather's nice."

"I can't. I've promised to go to San Juan Island with Hannah. She wants to visit some people that Debbie North talked to the day of her crash."

"Then let me take the two of you. A chaperoned trip. We can be together but can't be drawn into the *involvement* you keep talking about. How can you lose?"

Alexandra felt the pressure building behind her temples. This was the sort of thing she'd known to avoid and hadn't. Now she felt as if she were punishing Ben and punishing herself for having natural sexual urges and genuine feelings for each other. She didn't want it to be this way.

"Saturday it is," she said. "I'll tell Hannah."

"Do you want me to take you home now?"

"I'll grab a taxi."

"Don't you trust me?"

"I don't trust either of us."

"I'll lock up and walk you to the taxi stand."

The tension hovered between them as they left his office and took the elevator to the first floor. He walked her to the taxi area, then took her arm and tugged her around to face him. "I don't want to lose you before we have a chance to see how we'd be together. I want you to think about hypnotherapy. Dr. Abrams wouldn't have suggested it if he didn't think it had a good chance of being effective."

"I'll see Dr. Abrams again, but I'll have to think about the hypnosis."

"I guess I'll have to settle for that—for now."

"Don't expect miracles, Ben. Even Dr. Abrams didn't promise that."

"I'm due a miracle. You are, too."

She rose to her tiptoes and kissed him lightly on the cheek, then crawled into the back seat of a waiting cab. Miracles might happen in Ben's world. In hers, it was terror that was always just a breath away.

SATURDAY STARTED OUT as a beautiful day. The wind was relatively calm, the sun a huge ball of gold suspended in an incredibly blue sky. The air was so clear that the mountain was out, a favorite Seattle expression that meant that the whipped-cream peaks of Mount Rainier were visible in the distance.

But none of that eased Hannah's mind as they left the dock at Shilshole Marina and began the trip to San Juan Island. Her mother's boat was docked at the same marina, though it hadn't been there today. Apparently, Olivia and Drake were out for a cruise. Hannah hoped she wouldn't run into the couple on San Juan.

The island itself was familiar territory. Her parents had built a vacation home there when she was still in diapers. They had pictures of her toddling in the snow during one of the rare snowfalls that visited the area, and playing in the sand on a day much like this one. And she could actually remember holidays when all three families had stayed in the sprawling island house—Alexandra, Katherine and Hannah sharing the big bedroom with the alcove that looked out over Puget Sound.

The house had ended up on Olivia's side of the ledger during the divorce, as so many things had. Hannah's father, Kenneth, had been exceedingly generous. She doubted he would have been if he'd known the full truth about his wife.

But then, Hannah wondered if anyone really knew Olivia Brawney Richards. The many faces of Olivia. Hannah hoped she wasn't about to discover a new one today.

"I THINK WE SHOULD have lunch before we start making our appointed rounds," Ben said as they left the San Juan marina where he'd moored his boat. "There's a fish and chips place a couple of blocks from here. Nothing fancy, but the fish are fresh and the potatoes are crisp. Hard to beat that combination. And they have terrific salads."

"I could go for a bite to eat," Alexandra agreed. "I missed breakfast. Didn't even get my double chocolate latte with skim foam from Hy's."

"Now that's suffering," Ben said.

"I think I'll pass," Hannah said. "Jack made blueberry waffles for breakfast, and I'm still stuffed."

"And I guess he served them in bed," Alexandra said, teasing.

This time Hannah managed a genuine smile. "As a matter of fact, he did. So while you two are munching, I'll start with a visit to Margie Simmons."

"Was she the first person on Debbie's list?"

"No. She was the last. I thought I'd do this backward."

"Why don't you sit with us, Hannah?" Ben invited. "If you're not hungry, you can just have something to drink and then we'll all go to see Mrs. Simmons together."

"I appreciate the offer, but I'll do fine on my own for this visit. I've been to the house before. Margie and Mother are friends, and Margie's daughter Cherry and I took tennis lessons together every summer for years."

Besides, as much as she dreaded what she had to do, she wanted it over with. She had to know if what Debbie North had discovered linked Olivia to an antique crystal cross that had been stolen from the church the night Father Michael Cleary was murdered.

"YOU LOOK TERRIFIC, Hannah," Margie said, leading her through the house and onto the sundeck that overlooked a garden of colorful annuals, and beyond that a sailboat-dotted cove. "Marriage and pregnancy must be agreeing with you."

"So you've talked to Mother."

"I ran into her while John and I were having dinner at Downriggers a couple of weeks ago. She was with a new beau—a younger guy, nice-looking and very muscular. I can't remember his name, but he seemed nice. Not that he got a chance to say much. Olivia was in top form, looking magnificent and full of talk of her new motor yacht. I never thought I'd see her that excited about a boat."

"Mother is full of surprises."

"She always has been. And how is Kenneth? We never see him anymore."

"Dad's fine."

They talked for a few minutes, getting the preliminaries out of the way before Hannah could ask the questions that were plaguing her. She was just about to take the plunge when Margie excused herself, went into the house and came back carrying a tray of chicken salad sandwiches and glasses of iced green tea.

Hannah took one look at the food, then turned away quickly. Her stomach was as jumpy as her mind. Even at breakfast, she'd barely touched her waffles, resisting Jack's prompting.

"Hope you haven't had lunch," Margie said. "I had my housekeeper fix us a snack."

"I just ate," Hannah lied, "but the tea looks refreshing." She took a sip, then returned the glass to the tray that rested on a white garden table. "This isn't solely a social call, Margie."

"I thought that might be the case when you phoned. You sounded upset. Does this have something to do with that reporter who's been doing all the articles on you and the others connected to NorPac and Aerotech?"

"As a matter of fact, it does."

"I told John when she came out here asking me all those questions about some items I picked up at Olivia's garage sale that she was going to make more trouble for Olivia. Those reporters are always snooping around, digging for dirt."

"Did you know that Debbie North was killed in an accident?"

"No. I'm sorry to hear that. If I'd known, I wouldn't have made that comment about her. John says it's bad luck to criticize the dead."

"It's okay. Debbie would have taken your comment as a compliment. Snooping is a basic part of an investigative reporter's job." Snooping and searching for the truth, no matter where it led. Just as Hannah was doing now.

"Was one of the items you bought at Mother's garage sale an antique crystal cross with some unusual etching on the edges?"

Margie tilted her head and raised her eyebrows. "How did you know?"

"A lucky guess. Can I see it?"

"I don't have it anymore. Debbie said it was sold accidentally, that it was the property of one of the churches in Seattle. The story sounded fishy to me, but she gave me twice what I'd paid for it, so I didn't quibble. I mean, what kind of person would I be if I kept an icon that belonged to the Catholic church?"

What kind of person indeed? The anxiety that had haunted Hannah for days built to a crescendo.

"I called Olivia and told her that the North woman had been out here," Margie said, "and that she took the cross. If she was going to cause Olivia any trouble, I thought I should warn her first."

"What did Mother say when you told her?"

"She said she had no idea where the cross had come from, but that she'd probably picked it up at an art auction or purchased it from one of her suppliers for a client who'd decided not to take it. She didn't think it was valuable, though it looked as if it could be."

"Then she wasn't upset?"

"Not at all. Now, why don't you tell me all about that new husband of yours?"

"I'd love to, but I came to the island with some friends and I have to meet them in a few minutes. Perhaps another time."

"I hope so. Call me next time you're going to be

on the island visiting Olivia. Perhaps Cherry can come down from Vancouver for the day, and we can all get together for lunch. It will be just like old times.''

Hannah managed to get through the farewells and walk out of the house without showing visible signs of stress, but she knew she couldn't last much longer. Instead of walking back towards the restaurant where she was to meet Ben and Alexandra, she took the path down to the water's edge.

She needed a few moments alone and a chance to think about what she would do if she found that her mother actually was involved in the murder of a priest.

THE RESTAURANT was crowded, full of weekenders and locals who'd come out to enjoy the spectacular midsummer day. Ben and Alexandra opted for an outside table, one overlooking the marina. Ben ordered the house specialty, fish and chips. Alexandra ordered a salad and an iced coffee.

''I'm glad you let me tag along,'' he said as they waited for the food.

''Cheap transportation,'' she teased.

Alexandra's mood surprised him. Either salt air made her more laid back or she'd just managed to put some of her problems behind her for the day. Either way, he was grateful.

''I know this isn't a business trip,'' she said once the waitress had brought their drinks, ''but dare I ask how your purchase plans for the day care are going?''

''Moving right along.''

''Will you keep the current staff? They're all efficient and really good with the children.''

This was the opening he'd been waiting for. "I've been wanting to talk to you about staffing," he said, planning his approach as he talked.

"The teachers at Forrester Square are experienced, but there's always more to learn. The University of Washington has an excellent teacher education program, and they frequently offer seminars on child-care topics. And—"

"I'm sure the teachers are fine," he interrupted. "I'm more concerned about having the right supervisor."

"Hannah offered to help you find someone."

"I know, but I haven't given up on that someone being you."

She looked away, focused on a fisherman unloading his morning's catch. When she turned back to Ben, her eyes had lost their sparkle. "You know I can't make that kind of commitment."

"But if things work out, if your sessions with Dr. Abrams work the miracle I'm hoping for, would you be interested?"

"I'd jump at the chance if things were different."

"That's good enough for me." He reached across the table and took her hands in his. "I'll wait as long as it takes, Alexandra. For the satellite center and for you."

"Are you sure you're for real, Ben Jessup?"

"Go back to the boat with me and I'll show you how real I can be." He watched the blush creep to her cheeks and felt his body harden as desire stirred inside him.

"I'd love to. You know that."

But it wasn't going to happen. She thought that avoiding physical involvement would save him from pain and suffering if the nightmares didn't stop and she decided to run again. But it was too late to save him.

He was already in too deep.

IT WAS LATE AFTERNOON by the time Alexandra and Hannah joined Ben on the bridge of *Doug's Delite* for the ride back to Seattle. They'd taken advantage of the beautiful day and being on the island once Hannah had told them she'd decided not to visit the other people on the list. Hannah knew they assumed she had changed her mind because she'd been unsuccessful with Margie. She hadn't told them differently. No use to ruin their day as well as hers.

But it was time to level with them. "I know where the antique crystal cross is," she said. That got their attention, and she gave the account of her visit with Margie Simmons as calmly as she could manage.

"I'm sure there must be a reasonable explanation for this," Alexandra said as soon as Hannah stopped talking. "Your mother probably picked up the cross just as she told Margie—at an auction or from one of her suppliers."

"I hope you're right. Only..." Hannah let her words trail into silence.

"We'll be back in the city by seven," Ben said, "unless the wind picks up and slows us down. Why don't we stop at Our Lady of Mercy and talk to Father Dom about this? If Debbie took the cross to a church, as she told Margie she was going to do, she surely took it back to Our Lady of Mercy. For all we know, she may have gotten there and discovered it wasn't the cross that was stolen that night."

"I hate to keep you two any later," Hannah said. "I can visit Father Dom by myself."

"I think we should all go," Ben said. "We started this together. We should see it through. Now, let's relax and enjoy the ride back. There are snacks in the galley. Cheese, crackers, fruit, some pâté I picked up on the island while you two were having your latte break. And there's a bottle of wine or two in the bar."

"I'll get the snacks," Hanna said, already up and heading to the steps that led down to the galley.

Alexandra lingered behind, wanting a few seconds alone with Ben. "Thanks for today and for offering to drive by Our Lady of Mercy on the way home. You really are quite a terrific guy."

"Can I have that in writing?"

"In red ink."

She stood, ready to go help Hannah get the food and wine. He grabbed her hand as she did and held it tight. "Forget the ink. Just stay around for the next hundred years and tell me how terrific I am."

She was trembling as she descended the steps to the galley. Life in Seattle was growing more difficult by the day. So was avoiding Ben's touch. And his kisses. And dealing with a hunger for him that grew more intense every time they were together.

But she'd keep up her guard as long as she had to. Not for herself, but for Ben. And for Doug.

OUR LADY OF MERCY was tucked away in the Queen Anne district of historic homes and lush gardens, some hidden behind high stone walls. Alexandra knew it was the church the Kinards, the Richardses and her own family had attended back when they all owned houses surrounding Forrester Square.

Hannah had a picture of the families standing in front of the sanctuary one Christmas Eve. The three girls had been dressed in matching patent shoes and green-velvet dresses trimmed in white lace. And a smiling Father Michael Cleary had stood just behind them, sandwiched between Olivia and Helen Kinard.

Alexandra had purposely stayed away from this church since returning to Seattle, and she felt uneasy as the three of them stepped through the doors and into the vestibule. Six o'clock Saturday mass had apparently just ended. The pews were empty, but families and groups of friends were standing around in small clusters, talking and laughing.

"That's Father Dom," Ben said, pointing to the robed figure talking to an elderly lady about midway down the nave.

The priest was short and stocky, with snow-white hair and a balding pate.

"I'll tell him we'd like to talk to him privately," Ben said. He was stopped twice on his way to speak to Father Dom. From the way people smiled when Ben approached, it was easy to tell he was not only well known but well liked. Even Father Dom looked glad to see him at first, but the priest's mouth twisted into a frown when he turned to stare at Hannah and Alexandra.

"He said we can wait in the chancellery," Ben said when he rejoined them.

"Did you mention the crystal cross?" Hannah asked, her voice strained.

Alexandra felt a sudden rush of apprehension. Her gut instinct insisted Hannah was wrong about Olivia having any ties to the murder, but Hannah was more nervous than Alexandra had ever seen her. This strain couldn't be good for her friend's pregnancy.

She took Hannah's hand. "Maybe we shouldn't do this."

"We're here," Ben said. "And Father Dom may be able to clear everything up. Why shouldn't Hannah talk to him?"

Leave it to Ben to be practical and optimistic. Alexandra admired the qualities in him, but she didn't share them, probably because every time she found an answer, it only created more frightening questions.

"Ben's right," Hannah agreed, though she was holding on tightly to Alexandra's hand. "I set out to follow Debbie's steps and see what she'd wanted to tell me the night she died. My mission hasn't changed."

And so the three of them walked together through the beautiful old church, a place of prayer and reverence where people came to find peace and hope. Alexandra expected to find neither tonight.

CHAPTER ELEVEN

FATHER DOM sensed the tension that permeated the room the second he entered. He wasn't sure what this was about, but he feared that it was connected to the antique crystal cross that had been stolen from the church so many years ago and finally returned. The cross itself had made him nervous. When he'd touched the icon, he'd felt as if he were touching death itself, and he'd turned, almost expecting Father Michael to appear.

He felt that way again tonight, likely because he'd overheard just enough of the phone call Debbie North had made as she was leaving the chancellery to know that the person she'd called was Hannah.

"It's a joy to finally meet you, Alexandra," he said, extending his hand. "I've heard about you from Olivia and Helen and Louis Kinard."

"Thank you, Father Dom. I hope it was good things you heard."

"They're very fond of you. And it's very nice to see you again, Hannah."

"Thank you, Father Dom."

"And it always warms my heart to have a visit from you, Dr. Jessup. How's your son?"

"Doug is great, just growing up too fast."

"They do have a way of doing that, don't they? My sister makes the same complaint about her great-grandchildren.'' He turned back to Hannah, sensing that she was anxious and impatient. ''I trust Olivia is well.''

''She was the last time I talked with her.''

''Good. Your mother is most generous with her contributions. She has a remarkable faith, seeks forgiveness and accepts it with such childlike innocence that I have to fight the sin of envy that I'm not more like her.''

He tugged at his collar, which felt unusually stiff tonight, and straightened his robe. ''But you didn't come here tonight to talk about your mother, did you?''

''No. I came to ask if you'd talked to Debbie North before her death.''

So his assumption had been correct. ''Yes. Miss North was here just a few hours before she was killed in that horrible crash.''

''Did she bring you an icon that had been stolen from the church the night Father Michael Cleary was killed?''

''Yes. She returned the cross to us, but asked that I keep its return a secret until she had time to talk to a few people. I agreed.''

''Are you certain it's the same cross?'' Ben asked.

''The identification was verified. I'll have to go to the police with the information, since the theft occurred in connection with a murder. Debbie understood that. She only asked for a few days' grace. I would have already called them, except that I left on a trip to visit my sister the day after the cross was returned. I only arrived back in town this afternoon. But I must call the police tomorrow.''

''Perhaps you should call them tonight,'' Ben said.

"The murder of a priest is serious business, even if the crime was committed years ago."

"This is true." Once again he turned to Hannah, curious and apprehensive as to what her connection to the cross might be. "How did you know about the cross? Did Debbie tell you she'd returned it to the church?"

"No," Hannah said. "I hadn't talked to Debbie for several days before her death. I just slid a few pieces of a puzzle into place, the way the police will do."

"And when the pieces all fit, I hope we have Father Michael's killer in custody," he said.

"I hope so, too," Hannah agreed.

"Is there something else I can help you with?"

"No, Father," Hannah said. "But thank you for answering my questions."

"I'm glad I could help, but you seem upset. Are you sure you don't want to stay and talk awhile?"

"No. I'll be fine."

He walked with them a few feet, then watched as they strode down the narrow hallway to the door that led to the parking lot. Both Ben and Alexandra seemed subdued, but Hannah was clearly upset. He prayed she had nothing to do with the theft of the cross. News like that would deeply hurt her mother.

"IT'S BEEN A STRANGE DAY," Alexandra said as Ben walked her to the side entrance to her apartment. "I don't think I've ever seen Hannah so anxious. You don't think there's a chance Olivia actually had something to do with the theft of the cross, do you?"

"I wouldn't rule it out, and I don't think the police will, either."

"Olivia isn't short on faults, but she's very religious. She wouldn't have killed a priest."

"No, but she might have been fencing for thieves, taking stolen merchandise and selling it to clients as imports."

"I hadn't thought of that," Alexandra admitted. "If that's so, Debbie may have found proof that Olivia was dealing in stolen property. That could be why she was trying to reach Hannah the night she died in the car crash."

"Hopefully that won't turn out to be the case."

Alexandra fit her keys into the new double-bolt locks that Ben had installed. "I'm hoping for the best for Hannah's sake, but I'm too tired to think about it anymore tonight."

"Is that my cue to leave?"

She shook her head. "I'm not trying to be difficult, but I don't know what to do about us, Ben. I should never have let us become so close, but now that we have, I'm not sure staying apart is helping."

"It's definitely not helping me, but I won't push tonight. I know you're exhausted and need your rest, and I need to get home and relieve Mrs. Harold. But I do have something I want you to think about."

"As long as it's not murder or stolen religious icons."

"Nothing so morbid. Doug's birthday is next Saturday. Well, it's not actually his birthday. He was born Christmas week, but he was sick on his birthday and with the holiday approaching, I suggested we postpone and have a party when he turned three-and-a-half."

"I heard. He's having a party with ponies."

"And at least a dozen friends, mostly from the day care, but a few from the neighborhood."

"Sounds fun."

"So will you come? Doug would love to have you." He took her hands in his. "So would I."

She closed her eyes. A birthday party. Such a simple thing. Ponies, kids, ice cream and cake. She imagined herself walking up to the front door of the house at Forrester Square East—and then falling to pieces.

"I don't dare risk a visit to that house."

"It's not the one you lived in, Alexandra. You know that."

"But it's in the same spot and it's so similar."

"Always the past. You're a puppet and it's your master. And still you haven't agreed to hypnosis."

"I don't see how it could help for me to relive the fire."

"You do that anyway in the nightmares. If there are memories that you've repressed, they might be released in hypnosis."

"I wish the memories were repressed, instead of performing nightly for my macabre entertainment. But I'll think about it."

"Good. Now take care and get some sleep. I'll call you in the morning."

She ached to slide into his arms, to hold him close. Instead she rushed up the stairs, opened her door and stepped into yet another living nightmare.

The room was lit with the eerie glow of dozens of candles. They were everywhere. Large red ones on the coffee table. A cluster of small blue ones on top of the television set. Slender white tapers scattered among the books on the bookshelf. And one in the shape of a small dog resting on the windowsill, the flames dangerously close to the sheer curtains that fluttered around them.

In spite of the change in locks, someone had walked in, someone with a set of her new keys. As if in a trance, she flicked on the light and went from candle to candle, extinguishing the fluttering flames.

When she reached the ones on the bookcase, she discovered the photograph of the three families, the one she'd shown Gary Devlin a few days ago. It was out of the frame, propped against the one candle that had not been lit.

The Kinards, the Richardses and the four children were still smiling from the photograph, but Jonathan and Carrie Webber and Mr. Wiggles had been burned from the picture. The edges of the photograph were curled, as if it had been held in the candle's flame until nothing was left of Alexandra's parents or her pet shar-pei.

She clutched the bookcase, dizzy and nauseous. Why was this happening? What had she done to make someone so determined to drive her away?

And then a jolt of fury hit, so strong it overrode the terror. She'd run from the past and maybe from the truth all her adult life, but she'd never had anyone else call the shots. And she wouldn't start now.

Perhaps Dr. Abrams was right and there were secrets locked inside her mind, things that some cruel and twisted individual was afraid she would recall. Twenty-one years of nightmares hadn't brought the secrets to light. Hypnosis probably wouldn't do it, either.

But it might be the only chance she had.

HANNAH TALKED her latest plan over with Jack on Sunday afternoon. He didn't necessarily agree with her decision to hire a private detective to investigate her mother's background, but he understood, and that meant a lot.

Her first thought had been to call Olivia to ask her why there was no record of her attending, much less graduating from, Smith College. But she knew it would be a waste of time. Her mother would lie, and do it so convincingly that it would be difficult not to take her at her word.

It would be the same if she asked her about the crystal cross. Olivia would offer a perfectly reasonable explanation, or else deny knowing anything about it and appear shocked that she'd had a stolen religious icon in her possession. Hannah knew only too well that Olivia was the master of everything but the truth.

Flipping through the Yellow Pages of the Seattle phone book, Hannah found the listing for private investigators. This time she was reluctant to ask her friend Dylan Garrett for help. His agency, Finders Keepers, had found her son, and she knew Dylan would be happy to recommend a reliable P.I. in Seattle. But for the time being, she preferred as few people as possible to know what she was doing.

She read the names, hoping one would stand out. Everett George, licensed with ten years' experience. Reasonable fees. That pretty much covered it. Still, apprehension churned in her stomach as she picked up the receiver and dialed the number. Once she had the P.I.'s findings, she'd have to live with them—whatever they might be.

ALEXANDRA ARRIVED for her appointment with Dr. Abrams ten minutes before the scheduled time of five o'clock on Wednesday afternoon. Ben had wanted to come with her, but she'd refused his offer. Having him nearby, even if he weren't in the same room, would have made her more uncomfortable than she already was.

The waiting room was empty, and Hannah only sat for a couple of minutes before the nurse appeared at the side door.

"Dr. Abrams will see you now, Ms. Webber."

Alexandra's legs felt like lead as she stood and followed the nurse down a narrow corridor and into a room marked 3A. This room was smaller than the one she'd been in the last time. There was no desk in the room, only one overstuffed chair and a matching sofa. Soft music—something New Age and relaxing—and dim lighting gave the room a slightly surreal quality.

"Just have a seat on the coach, and try to relax," the nurse said. "Dr. Abrams will be with you shortly."

As she sat down, Alexandra closed her eyes, then jerked to attention a few seconds later when Dr. Abrams joined her.

"I'm glad you decided to do this, Alexandra."

She sucked in a deep breath and let it out slowly. "It was more or less decided for me."

"How is that?"

"Someone is determined I leave town, and I'm too stubborn to take orders. That's one of my biggest faults."

"Stubbornness can be a survival trait. It's probably kept you from falling into a serious depression and giving up in the face of fatigue and constant nightmares."

"Anyway, that's why I'm here, though I don't really see how hypnosis can help. It's not as if I don't remember what happened. The problem is that I can't stop remembering."

"You may be right. Hypnotherapy can be a valuable tool if used correctly, but it's not a cure-all. However, in your case, it's probably our best option."

"What should I expect? Will I just become unconscious and answer every question you ask me?"

"You won't be unconscious, but you will be in a more susceptible state than usual. I'll guide your thinking with questions. Hypnosis should allow you to increase your concentration and focus to the point where you are able to retrieve memories previously blocked from your conscious thought."

"Will I remember what I say once I come out from under the hypnosis?"

"Most people remember everything. On rare occasions, a person may have no recollection, but I'll try to keep that from happening by not letting you sink too deeply into the hypnotic state."

"How do we start? I don't see a gold watch for you to swing."

He smiled. "Sorry. I'm not quite as intriguing as movie and TV hypnotists. I lean more towards the subtle. Just try to relax and tell me what happened the night of the fire."

"Where do I start?"

"With whatever comes to your mind."

"I woke up and wished it was daybreak. I guess I've been doing that ever since." She closed her eyes and let the memories drift into her mind and take over. The sheets were cool as she tunneled under them and searched for Mary Jane.

JASPER ABRAMS LISTENED and ached for the frightened six-year-old that his patient had gradually become. Life had done a number on her, and if she couldn't get past this one night in her past, she'd never be whole again. "What do you see now, Alexandra?"

"Daddy is arguing with Mommy."

"What are they arguing about?"

She put her hands to her face and frowned, as if trying to remember. "I don't know, but Mommy is very, very mad. I'm being quiet now. I don't want her to see me. I think I must have done something very wrong to make Mommy and Daddy argue like this. Oh, no!"

"What happened?"

"I dropped Mary Jane and she fell through the railings. I want her back."

"Why don't you go and get her?"

"I'm afraid."

"What's happening now?"

"Daddy is holding a piece of paper over a burning candle. He shouldn't do that. It's making Mommy very mad. No! No! Mommy has a gun. She's going to shoot Daddy!" Alexandra rocked back and forth, then cupped her hands over her ears. "Make it stop. Make the clock stop making that noise."

"What kind of noise is it making?"

"Gong. Gong. Gong. *Gong!*"

"Four gongs?"

"No. The last one…"

"What happened on the last one?"

"It was too loud. It woke up Mommy."

"But your mother is in the living room with your dad."

"Not yet. She's running down the stairs, screaming at Daddy and me to get out of the house."

"Then who's in the living room?"

"Mommy and Daddy and... I don't know." Her voice rose to a near scream and she started clutching and clawing at her chest. "I can't breathe. There's too much smoke. It's so hot in here. Help me, Daddy. Please, help me. Daaaaddy!"

Jasper jumped from his chair, crossed the few feet between them and put a reassuring hand on Alexandra's arm. "It's okay, Alexandra. The fire is over. It's cool in here. The air is clear. And the grandfather clock is silent."

She pulled out of the trance instantly, though her breathing was short and choppy and perspiration beaded her forehead. She glanced around the room as if unsure of her surroundings, then focused her gaze on him.

"Did you see something new, Alexandra?"

She clasped and unclasped her hands. "A gun. My mother was holding a gun."

"Did she fire it?"

"I don't know, but she had it. It was a small pistol, dull black, but the handle was shiny."

"Did she shoot your father?"

"She couldn't have. He saves me from the fire. He holds me in his arms and tells me I'm all right. That always happens in my nightmares."

"Did he do that today?"

"No."

"You don't want to believe he's dead, do you?"

"You think my mother shot and killed my father that night, don't you?"

"Do you think that?"

"No. Why did you stop me so soon?"

"You were getting hysterical and we'd probably gone deep enough for the first session. Next time you may be able to handle it better."

"Then you think there's more that I've blocked from my mind."

"I do. There were still memories you were afraid to unleash."

"When can you see me again?"

"Next Monday. I'll tell the receptionist to make certain she fits you in."

"I appreciate that, though I don't know why you're going to such trouble for me."

"You need it. Besides, you're a friend of Ben's, and he and I go back all the way to our first year in med school. He's a supernice guy."

"I know."

He walked over to the table by the wall and poured a glass of water from a silver decanter. "Drink this," he said, placing the glass in her hand. "You should relax a few minutes before you leave."

"I will."

Jasper stayed with her until her breathing returned to normal and the frightened look had disappeared from her eyes. She'd been through a lot today, but she had worse horrors yet to face. He was certain of that.

ALEXANDRA STARTED WALKING, not paying any attention to where she was going, just feeling the need to keep moving. For the first few blocks, she felt numb, almost dazed. Then, slowly, every detail of today's session replayed in her mind. The new images were the most prominent. The pistol. Her mother running down the stairs and yelling for her and her father to get out of the house. Only her mother was already downstairs, pointing a pistol at her husband.

Alexandra was still walking aimlessly and thinking an hour later when her cell phone rang. It was probably Ben. He'd be worried about her.

"Hello?"

"Hello, Alexandra. This is Ernie Brooks. I hope you don't have important plans for this evening. I need to see you."

"Where are you?"

"At a hotel in Belltown. I flew in today from San Antonio."

"Is this about Gary Devlin?"

"No. It's about Jonathan Webber. I think it's time you know the truth about him. Is there somewhere we can meet and talk?"

"There's a coffeehouse in Belltown, near Forrester Square Day Care. I could meet you there in half an hour."

"Sounds good."

She gave him the directions to Caffeine Hy's, then broke the connection. The hits just never stopped. She hesitated for a few seconds, then dialed Ben's office number. With luck, she could catch him before he left.

Seeing him tonight was probably the worst thing she could do for both of them, but she couldn't face another round of frightening truths without his strength.

And that might be the scariest truth of all.

CHAPTER TWELVE

THE OUTDOOR TABLES at Caffeine Hy's were all taken. Alexandra scanned the area to see if Ben or Ernie had arrived before her. When she didn't see either of them, she went inside and found a small table at the back with room for the three of them. Hannah had agreed to drop Doug off at Mrs. Harold's so that Ben could stay as long as needed.

"The usual?" the waitress asked, stopping at her table.

"Not tonight, Nora. Just hot coffee, the strongest you have, and black."

"Bad day?"

"It could have been better."

Nora and Alexandra looked up as the door opened and Ben stepped inside. Nora smiled as Ben waved and strode towards them. "Looks like it's about to improve," she said.

Alexandra doubted it, but she wasn't going to explain the details of her convoluted life to someone she only knew from the coffeehouse.

Ben pulled out a chair next to hers, ordered black coffee, and scooted his chair closer. "I'm glad you called."

"I'm glad you came."

"I wanted to call you, but when I talked to Jasper, he said you'd left and wanted some time alone."

"I did. I spent the hour before Ernie called just walking and thinking."

"So why'd he fly out here from San Antonio to meet with you?"

"I haven't the slightest idea, except that he says it concerns my father."

"Are we talking Gary Devlin here or Jonathan Webber?"

"Jonathan."

The door opened again. A middle-aged couple walked in and right behind them was Ernie Brooks. "That's Ernie," she said. "The voice of truth."

"For what that's worth. In your situation, truth seems to have as many faces as Seattle has coffee-houses."

Ernie was short, but he was in great shape for a man who was well into Medicare. He still had a full head of hair, mostly gray, but with a nice peppering of brown. He was dressed in worn jeans, a cotton shirt and a pair of Western boots.

"Looks like a Texan," Ben said as Ernie acknowledged Alexandra with a tip of his Stetson before letting his gaze scan the rest of the room. "And acts like a lawman."

Alexandra dragged in a shaky breath as Ernie took the chair opposite hers. Today she'd remembered seeing a gun in her mother's hand. Now she had the disturbing suspicion she was about to find out why.

ERNIE SETTLED IN the skinny chair and looked into the soulful depths of Alexandra Webber's striking green eyes and felt like a real chump for the part he'd played in screwing up her life. So, whether the FBI liked it or not, he had to let her know she could be in real danger. He owed that to Jonathan Webber and to his own peace of mind.

"Thanks for seeing me, Alexandra."

"I could hardly refuse when you told me the topic of discussion."

She shook his hand and held it for a second, then introduced him to the guy sitting next to her. Ernie would have preferred talking to her alone, but it didn't matter much. Once he said his piece, she could tell anybody she wanted to, anyway.

He ordered a black coffee and wished he was back in San Antonio having a beer with his buddies. But he was here, so he might as well get on with it. "I've been thinking about what you're going through, Alexandra, and I decided there were a couple of things you deserve to know about your father."

She didn't say a word, but he could read the troubled look in her eyes.

"It's nothing bad," he assured her. "In fact, it's just the opposite. Jonathan Webber was a great guy. He stood up for what he believed in."

Alexandra leaned in closer. "How did you know my father?"

"He helped me out on a case once."

"What case?"

"The one involving Eagle Aerotech."

"My father was one of the owners of Eagle Aerotech."

"Which was why we needed his help in finding out who was responsible for selling the software illegally."

"Are you saying my father helped convict Louis Kinard?"

"We already had solid evidence against Kinard,

but not enough to guarantee us a conviction. We needed an inside source for that. You father agreed to be that man.''

Alexandra's eyes turned an even deeper green, her gaze more intent. ''But everyone says my dad and Louis were like brothers.''

''It was a serious crime, Alexandra. That software in the wrong hands could cost American lives. Your father did what he thought was right. It takes a big man to do that.''

''Let me get this straight,'' Ben said. ''You're saying Jonathan Webber did the undercover work for the FBI's case?''

''Not all of it. He cooperated with us.''

Ben kicked back from the table and studied Ernie, no doubt wondering if he actually had his facts straight. ''He cooperated with you to get the goods on Kinard. Then his house caught fire and he and his wife were burned to death the night before Louis was arrested. I guess you're going to say that was all just an unfortunate coincidence.''

''I couldn't swear to that, but I do know the FBI had nothing to do with the fire,'' Ernie said, thankful it was the truth.

Ben pushed his coffee cup aside. ''But someone could have set the fire—someone who wanted to keep Jonathan Webber from talking. And if that someone else just happened to be in the house that night, then Alexandra is the only one still alive who might have seen them.''

Ben Jessup caught on real fast.

''But Louis Kinard was found guilty, and he's already served his time,'' Alexandra said.

''Served time for selling software,'' Ben reminded

her. ''Not for setting a fire that killed two people. And there is no statute of limitations on murder.''

''I don't think you can necessarily push this all Kinard's way,'' Ernie said. ''Louis was the only one convicted, but he may not have been the only one involved in the crime.''

''So there's no telling who might have started that fire?''

''I'd say that's pretty much the scenario,'' Ernie said.

Ben reached over and took Alexandra's hand. ''Bottom line is that Alexandra could be in real danger and the FBI isn't doing a damn thing about that.''

''That's why I wanted to level with you.''

''There was another crime committed that night,'' Ben said.

''Are you talking about the priest who was murdered?''

''So you know about that?''

''The FBI was aware of that murder,'' Ernie admitted. ''We checked to see if the two were connected. There wasn't the slightest bit of evidence to indicate that they were.''

They talked a few more minutes, though there was really nothing else Ernie could say. He had warned Alexandra. That was all he could do without being guilty of a very serious breach of FBI policy. When he finished his coffee, he stood and pulled his wallet from his back pocket.

''I've got it,'' Ben said. ''But what's your rush?''

''I'm meeting someone else in a half hour.''

Alexandra looked up at him. ''So you didn't fly to Seattle just to tell me this about my father?''

''Not entirely.''

"Can I call you if I have more questions?" she asked.

"You can call, but I don't know what else I can tell you."

"What about Gary Devlin?" she asked. "When you came before, you told me to follow my heart and you called me 'Kitten.' Kitten was my father's name for me."

"I guess I must have heard him call you that and it stuck with me. As for Gary Devlin, I'd take the FBI's advice and stay the hell away from him for now. Take care of yourself. If your dad were here, he'd likely tell you the same thing. Look, I really have to go."

"Thanks for coming."

Ernie shook Ben's hand and walked out before Alexandra thought of another question. He had a meeting with the local cop who'd run Devlin's fingerprints. And then Ernie was off to find Gary Devlin for a long overdue reunion. Apparently the Alzheimer's had made Gary forget most of his life. Ernie suspected there were worse things that could happen to men like the two of them.

BEN SAT in the coffeehouse, his insides a mass of jangled nerves as Alexandra filled him in about her session with Jasper and the burning candles and damaged photograph she'd discovered after he'd left Saturday night.

"Why didn't you tell me all that when it happened?" Ben demanded, not knowing whether he wanted to hold her or to shake her.

"Because I can't keep dragging you into my problems. I shouldn't have called you today."

"You never drag me into your problems. I volunteer. Hell, I practically beg to be used. Do you think I want to sit by and do nothing while some dangerous lunatic breaks into your apartment?"

"I don't know what you can do about it. I reported it to the police the next day. They checked for fingerprints on the lock and the photo but didn't find any."

"They didn't find any on the gasoline-soaked rag or the bag it came in, either."

"So all I can do is keep seeing Dr. Abrams and hope I'll remember something that will make sense of all of this."

"You could move in with me in the meantime, at least until your landlord and his wife return from vacation."

She looked at him as if he'd lost his mind. "You know I can't stay in that house."

"Don't tell me you're more afraid of a house than a madman."

"I just can't stay in that house."

"Then I'll stay with you at your apartment."

"You can't do that, either. You have Doug." She exhaled sharply and stared him down. "This is exactly why I tried not to get involved with you, Ben. It's why I've never let anyone get too close. My whole life is a literal nightmare."

She started to tremble. Ben tried to put his arms around her shoulders, but she pulled away.

"You should go home, get your running shoes and run away from me as fast and as far as you can, Ben Jessup."

"I'm not afraid of a few nightmares, Alexandra." But he was afraid. He'd lost one woman he'd loved and he was scared to death of losing again. He stood and tugged Alexandra to her feet. He had to find some way to keep her safe. Only problem was, he had no earthly idea how he'd handle that task.

"WANT ME TO GET that, hon?"

"That's okay, Jack. I've got it." Hannah fit the lid over the fresh green beans and grabbed for the kitchen extension. She hoped it was Alexandra, calling to say how her meeting with Ernie Brooks went, but more likely it was Olivia. She'd called the center twice today, but Hannah hadn't taken the calls. She just wasn't ready to deal with her mother yet. "Hello? McKay residence. You're talking to the cook."

"Can I speak to Mrs. McKay?"

It was neither Alexandra nor Olivia. She couldn't place the voice, but it sounded familiar. "I'm Mrs. McKay. How can I help you?"

"This is Everett George, the private investigator you hired to check out Olivia Brawney Richards."

She exhaled slowly. "Do you have news for me already?"

"Quite a bit. I'm writing up a report for you, but since you seemed in a hurry to get the information, I thought I'd call."

"I appreciate that. What did you uncover?"

"Are you sure you want to know? That probably sounds like a strange question since you paid me to go snooping, but I always ask in cases like this. People think they want to know, but sometimes they really don't. You get my drift?"

Hannah leaned against the door facing, suddenly flooded with doubts. No matter what Everett told her, her mother would be her mother, so perhaps it would be better not knowing. But there was still the matter of the cross. Her hands tightened on the receiver. "I want to know."

She listened silently as Everett spun a tale of deceit and lies that went back to before her parents met. The Olivia Brawney whom Everett believed Olivia Richards to be grew up in New Mexico as an only child in a single-parent home. Her mother had been sickly when Olivia was growing up, and the family had existed mostly on welfare and the generosity of the local church.

Olivia had spent her teenage years working with her mother in a roadside convenience store—Mendos Supermart. She left home at twenty-one, and no one in her hometown had heard from her since. Her mother currently lived in a subsidized apartment in the same neighborhood where Olivia had grown up.

"I can fly down to New Mexico and check out the story if you like," Everett said, "but I can pretty much guarantee the facts I gave you are accurate."

"Just give me Mrs. Brawney's current address." It was years too late, but she should meet her grandmother face-to-face.

ERNIE WAS WAITING in front of the hotel when Griffin drove up in a late-model, black Honda. Griffin stopped, then reached across the seat and opened the passenger side door.

"You must be Ernie Brooks."

"And I guess that would make you Griffin Frazier."

"You got it. Climb in. If we're going to talk about Gary Devlin, we may as well do it on his turf."

''In the underground tunnels?'' Ernie asked, climbing in and closing the door behind him.

''Why not? We can stroll around the area first, give you a feel for the place. The city's trying to bring the whole area back. They've made progress. New businesses have come in. Lots of the old ones have been spruced up, but the homeless still think of it as theirs.''

''Guess everyone has to have some place to call home.''

''Yeah. Even men like Gary Devlin. Any chance you're going to tell me what he's done that gets him special attention from the Bureau?''

''It's classified.''

''Is he dangerous?'' Griffin asked.

''He's not in jail.''

''Lots of dangerous men aren't in jail.''

Ernie saw the lights from the baseball stadium. Apparently the Mariners were in town. The bay was to his left and he could see a couple of Washington State ferries and a huge cruise ship docked nearby before they turned right onto Columbia Street.

''I know you Bureau guys like to flaunt that classified crap, but you're no better than us,'' Griffin said as he turned left onto a side street. ''City cops, FBI, CIA. It's all about law enforcement and protecting the citizens.''

''I'm not in the Bureau anymore,'' Ernie said. ''Haven't been for years.''

''So give me the scoop on Gary Devlin.''

''He's an old man suffering from Alzheimer's.''

''Then why are you here looking for him?''

''He's also an old friend. I'd like to see him again.'' And help him if he needed it, but that wasn't for Griffin to know. "When was the last time you saw him?"

"Last week. But someone besides Alexandra is looking for him. I figured it was one of the Bureau's guys."

"How do you know someone's looking for him?"

"Homeless guys gossip like everyone else. They say a young muscular type in a Seattle Seahawk cap has been asking questions."

"But as far as you know, the person who was looking for Devlin hasn't found him?"

"No. Devlin could be anywhere. There are miles of tunnels under the old part of the city. It would be tough on a stranger to know where to begin looking."

But an experienced cop like Griffin with his ear to the gossip mill could probably locate the man. "Tell you what, Griffin, you help me find Gary Devlin and I'll see that he leaves your area."

"That's a deal."

Only they'd have to move fast. Ernie had a strong suspicion that if he didn't find Devlin before the man in the Seahawk cap did, he'd be visiting the poor guy in the Seattle morgue.

ONCE DOUG WAS TUCKED IN for the night, Ben changed to his shorts and headed for his third-floor exercise room. Nothing like pushing his body to the limit to relieve stress. He did a dozen push-ups, then started working with his weights.

The muscle strain and sweat had little effect on the troublesome thoughts that occupied his mind tonight. He knew diseases, syndromes, viruses and infections. He could name all the major antibiotics and tell you which ones worked best on which symptoms and what side effects to look for.

He didn't know beans about the FBI or police investigations, and he definitely didn't understand how so many secrets existed in a world overrun with lawyers and investigative reporters. But he was fairly certain of a couple of things.

One, the case involving Louis Kinard and Aerotech was far from being solved. And, two, the fire that burned down the Webber home was not an accident. The timing was too critical. Seattle's mighty three had been falling faster than an avalanche and carrying their families down with them.

The fire had to be a case of arson, deliberately and intentionally set either to stop Jonathan Webber from gathering more information or to punish him for cooperating with the FBI. Unless…

He set the weights down and straddled a padded bench as a darker scenario came to mind. Jonathan Webber might not have been the victim. He could be the one who sold the software. He could have fooled the FBI and set up his best friend to take the rap for him.

Carrie Webber might have found out about her husband's crimes and pulled a gun on him, just the way Alexandra had seen it happen while she was under hypnosis. In fact, Alexandra might have seen and heard all kinds of incriminating information while she'd huddled on the landing. If those were the memories she'd blocked from her mind, then he hated to think what facing the truth would do to her. But it could be worse—much worse.

Gary Devlin might actually be her father. He could have set the fire that killed his wife and then abandoned his daughter. He could be the person tormenting her with burning candles and gasoline-soaked rags, threatening her with death if she didn't leave town before she regained her memory of that night.

And if Ben's theory was correct, and Alexandra did remember, the truth would destroy her. But if she didn't remember, the nightmares would continue, and she'd walk away from him and any chance they had of having a future together.

If Jonathan Webber was guilty, there was absolutely no way for him or Alexandra to win.

ALEXANDRA FELT TOTALLY drained when she finally climbed into bed. Ben had been wonderful, as usual. He'd insisted on hiring someone to watch her apartment. The cop was out there now, parked somewhere in the dark, watching her entrance. And she had his pager number. All she had to do was call and he'd be here in a matter of seconds.

Ben had wanted to stay the night, but she'd made him leave. Doug needed his father. And as much as she liked being with Ben, she needed time to herself to think about all she'd learned from her session with Dr. Abrams and from Ernie Brooks.

The thoughts roamed her mind in no particular order until she was so tired she couldn't bring any of them into clear focus.

She was tired, so very tired. Perhaps tonight the nightmare would take a break. The last thing she saw before she closed her eyes was Mary Jane, perched on the corner of her dresser, her black glass eyes staring at Alexandra.

"DON'T DO IT, Mommy. Don't shoot Daddy."

But she pointed the gun right at him. And then the

clock started to gong. One. Two. Three. She cupped her hands over her ears, but the fourth gong was the loudest of all. Blood spurted from the man as he fell to the floor. Oh, no! Oh, no! Oh, no! Daddy was dead. And the fire and smoke were everywhere.

"It's okay. I've got you, Kitten. Just hold on." Daddy picked her up and carried her outside into the cool night air. She wrapped her arms around him, but when she looked up, it wasn't Daddy. It was someone old and wrinkled. His beard was dirty and matted and he smelled like gasoline.

And all Alexandra could do was scream.

BEN JERKED AWAKE from a sound sleep, sure something was wrong. He walked down the hall and checked on Doug. His son was sleeping peacefully.

His mind flew to Alexandra as he walked to the kitchen for a glass of cool water, and a wave of dread washed over him. The kitchen clock said 2:00 a.m. She was home, her doors locked tight, but still he couldn't shake the eerie premonition that something was wrong.

He shouldn't call and wake her, yet he knew that even if she needed him, she wouldn't call. She'd proven that the other night when she'd found the burned photograph of her parents.

His muscles tightened into twisted coils. No matter what she thought, he had to make certain she was safe. Picking up the receiver to the cordless phone, he stepped out onto the patio so that the sound of his voice wouldn't wake Doug.

Alexandra answered on the first ring. And as soon as he heard her voice, he knew he'd been right to call. "What's wrong?" he asked, not even trying to hide the anxiety that was churning inside him.

"The nightmare." Her voice was hoarse, as if she'd been crying.

"I'm coming there, Alexandra."

"No. You have Doug."

"Mrs. Harold won't mind coming over. She does it when I have to go to the hospital for emergencies in the middle of the night."

"I'll be fine, Ben. It's just that..."

Her voice broke and he could all but see her standing there, shaking and tormented, determined to handle everything by herself. But this time he wasn't asking her permission. She needed him. And he was damn well going to be there for her.

There were some things a man had to do just because he couldn't help himself.

"I'll be there in half an hour—sooner if I can make it."

CHAPTER THIRTEEN

ALEXANDRA FELL into Ben's arms the instant he walked through the door. She'd gone against every rule she'd lived by when she'd let herself get involved with Ben, but she couldn't help herself tonight. He was here, and she'd never needed strong arms around her as much as she did tonight. Not just any arms. She needed Ben.

"I should have never left you alone tonight," he whispered. "Not after the session with Jasper and the meeting with Ernie Brooks."

"Oh, Ben, you can't protect me from my own life."

"I can try."

She held on tight. He was so warm, so real. She felt his breath on her neck, and something new and powerful stormed her senses. In spite of all she'd been through, all the pain, all the tension, she trembled with an ache that reached deep into her soul.

She tilted her head so that she met Ben's gaze, and the same need that consumed her seemed to be burning in his eyes. His lips were so close. If she raised herself a hairbreadth, they would be on hers. All she had to do was claim them. Still, she pulled away.

Only this time, Ben didn't let her go. He pulled her back into his arms, his breath ragged. "Why must you always fight us, Alexandra? There's so much else in your life to fight, why can't you just let me hold you without pushing me away?''

Let him hold her. Feel his body pressing against hers. Suck up his strength. Taste his kiss, all salty sweet and deliciously decadent. She wanted to. God, how she wanted to. In all her life she'd never known the kind of craving that drove her now.

''Because if I stay in your arms another second, I'm going to kiss you. And if I kiss you the way I'm feeling right now, Ben Jessup, I just may never let you go.''

And that was all the invitation Ben needed. His mouth closed on hers and she lost herself in the kiss—and in Ben. Passion exploded between them. Hot desire, compelling and wanton. His hands tangled in her hair and roamed her back as her body melded against his. She held nothing back, wasn't sure she could have even if she'd wanted.

But she didn't want to. If she was going to do this, she was going to do it right, and make memories that would last a lifetime.

''Make love with me, Ben.''

He trembled and thrust his hands in her hair once more. ''Are you sure? I want you so badly I can barely breathe, but I don't want you to have regrets.''

''No regrets. I promise.''

He picked her up and carried her across the floor and into the bedroom. ''Let me undress you,'' she whispered as he lowered her to the bed, then began to slip out of his shoes and socks.

''You are a constant surprise, Alexandra Webber.''

''Part of my charm.'' She stayed on the bed, balanced herself on her knees and fitted her hands beneath his T-shirt. She lifted it slowly, exposing his muscled chest inch by gorgeous inch.

"I could help," Ben said when she struggled to get the shirt over his head.

"Don't you dare." When the shirt was off, she dropped it to the floor and raked her fingers through the hair that matted his chest. The dark hairs curled around her painted fingernails, dark brown against a pale coppery shade of red, a mingling of colors and textures that took her arousal even higher. She buried her face in his chest, kissing and nibbling her way from his neck to his abdomen.

He moaned softly, and when she looked down, she saw the bulge pressing against the fabric of his shorts. A new, crushing wave of desire hit with mind-numbing force and she fit her hands under the legs of his shorts and worked her fingers upward until she touched his erection.

Slowly her fingers trailed and stroked him, until finally she stretched the elastic at his waist and tugged the shorts over his hips. He shuddered as she lowered herself and tasted the salty wetness.

When she pulled away, he kicked his boxers off completely and climbed into bed beside her. "My turn," he whispered hoarsely. "I'll try to keep a slow hand, but I'm not sure how long I can last."

He caught her mouth with his. The kiss was ravenous, his mouth hard and demanding, as if he couldn't get enough. Tugging the narrow straps of her cotton gown from her shoulders, he let his kisses slide down her neck while his hands cupped her breasts, his thumbs kneading her pebbled nipples. She let her hands roam and massage his back as he slid the gown down her legs and tossed it to the floor.

"You're beautiful, Alexandra. Soft. Warm. Perfect."

It was pillow talk, the kinds of things men said when they were lost in the throes of passion. She knew it, but still she loved hearing it. Loved the way he said her name and the feel of his lips on her bare skin.

Her need was all-consuming now, his touch so intoxicating that the outside world ceased to exist. There were only the two of them. No past. No future. No fear.

She arched towards him and he rolled against her, pulling her close. Her breasts melded against his muscled chest and her thighs pressed into his, the hard length of him pulsating between them.

"I never thought I would feel this way..."

She touched her fingers to his lips. "Don't talk, Ben. Please don't talk. Just make love with me. Make love like it's the last night of our lives."

She parted her thighs, took his erection in her hand and guided it to her. Passion raged inside her, driving her until she thought her body might explode.

And finally it did, carrying her right over the top with him. It was rockets and delirium, but also incredibly sweet and totally fulfilling.

She held on to him as he relaxed in her arms. The slick sheen of their lovemaking still warm between them, she buried her face in his chest so that she could feel the rapid beating of his heart and hear the sharp, quick pattern of his breathing.

For the first time in as long as she could remember, she felt contented and safe. At one with herself, and with a man who touched her heart the way no man ever had before. She felt as far away from the fear and nightmares as she could ever hope to be. And as she lay there quietly, she tried to memorize the feeling and the moment.

It might never come again.

MRS. BRAWNEY'S APARTMENT was a few miles north of Albuquerque, just off the highway in an area of older homes and crumbling buildings. Hannah stared at the four-plex as Jack pulled the rented car into the driveway.

"Six-twelve," Jack said. "That would make it the one on the right, first floor."

The complex was a pinkish stucco with gray shutters, much like others on the street. It needed some work, but it was livable. The yard was a hodgepodge of native plants and clumps of wild grasses, but annuals flourished in a couple of red clay pots, and two redwood rockers sat at odd angles on a narrow porch. A plaster statue of Mary guarded a small rock and cacti garden.

"I'm still hoping we find this is all a mistake and that the Olivia Brawney who was raised here was not my mother," Hannah said. "Not that I'd care if she'd been dirt poor all her life."

"I know. It's the deception that makes this difficult for you to take." He reached across the seat and squeezed her hand. "But you don't know anything for certain yet. The private investigator could have made a mistake."

"He seemed pretty sure of his facts," Hannah reminded Jack.

"Even if he's right, Olivia may have very good reasons for what she did."

"Yeah. Money, prestige, success, attention."

"She's not all bad," Jack said. "Olivia gives money to the church, and she loves you in her own peculiar way."

"Whose side are you on?"

"Yours, babe, all the way. And now that we have that settled, I think we should get out of the car and ring the doorbell." He opened his door. "Race you to the house."

"Think you can beat a pregnant woman, huh?"

"No doubt about it."

"Not this time, speed demon. We stick together. There's strength in numbers."

"You must be expecting one tough grandma to open that front door."

"Could be," Hanna said. "She gave birth to Mother."

"You've got a point there."

Hannah felt a little like a soldier storming the enemy hideout as she stepped onto the driveway. Ready or not, she was going in.

ANY ILLUSIONS Hannah had about being at the wrong house disappeared the second she came face-to-face with Dorothy Brawney. The resemblance was remarkable, even though Dorothy was even thinner than Olivia, and instead of perfectly coiffed and meticulously highlighted hair, hers was mostly gray, with split ends that jutted off in all directions. But the bone structure, skin tone, and even the shape of her eyes and nose reminded Hannah of her mother.

Dorothy Brawney bent over and picked up a gray house cat that was purring and wrapping itself around her ankles. "Whatever you're selling, I probably can't afford and don't need,'' she said, though her tone was friendly.

''Glad I'm not a struggling salesman,'' Jack replied. He smiled and offered his hand. ''We're Jack and Hannah McKay. I know you don't know us, but we're trying to track down a friend who used to live in this neighborhood.''

The woman shook his hand, but stared at Hannah. ''What's your friend's name?''

''Her last name is Brawney,'' Jack answered. ''We're hoping you might be a relative.''

''Not likely. I don't have any family around here.''

''We'd still like to talk, unless we caught you at a bad time.''

''Don't worry about that. When you get my age, time's about all you have. That and a lot of aches and pains. I'll be seventy-three in March.''

That would have made her a mere seventeen when Olivia was born, Hannah noted. Not much more than a child herself.

''You're a very youthful seventy-three,'' Jack said, smiling and turning on the charm.

Dorothy beamed. ''Thank you. It's all in the mind. Age, I mean. A woman is only as old as she feels.'' She opened the door a little wider. ''No use to stand out here in the heat. I know you can't be too careful of strangers these days, but you look honest, and I'm a good judge of people. I could always spot a shoplifter the minute one walked in the store. Mr. Mendos said I had a gift for picking out bad apples.''

''I'm glad we pass inspection,'' Jack said, ''but you really shouldn't open your doors to strangers.''

''Where are you folks from?''

''Seattle,'' Hannah said, finally managing to get her

wits about her enough to speak. "I've lived there all my life."

"I've always wanted to go up to the Northwest. I've got a daughter up there somewhere. At least I think that's where she is. She married some rich guy and I haven't heard from her in years. But you didn't come here to listen to me go on and on. Now you know all about me, so we're not strangers anymore." She motioned them to come in. "And if I keep holding this door open, all my air-conditioning is going to escape."

They followed her inside, and Hannah was hit again with the bizarre reality of the situation. She was halfway across the country, talking about a mother she didn't really know with a grandmother she hadn't known existed.

Hannah had thought emotions would take over at a time like this. Anger at her mother or a rush of warmth for Dorothy Brawney—something. Instead Hannah felt numb, as if her central nervous system had simply shut down.

"Have a seat," the woman said, "as long as you don't mind getting a few cat hairs on you. I've got three of them. All strays that wandered up hungry. What could I do but feed them? And once you do, they're yours for life. A lot more loyal than flesh and blood."

Hannah crossed the room and sat on the couch, but her gaze settled on a cluster of framed photographs on the far wall. There was no doubt that they were of Olivia. As a baby, as a scrawny preteen, and several of her as a thin but very attractive teenager. Her hair was brown when she was young, but by the time she was high school age, it had been lightened to an ash-blond, long and shiny and falling over bare shoulders.

"So who is this Brawney woman you're looking for? If she lives around here, chances are I know her. I worked at Mendos Supermart for almost forty years, right up until my arthritis got so bad I couldn't take standing up all day. Everybody around here stops in there from time to time."

Hannah took a deep breath. She'd found out what she needed to know, and she didn't want to be here under false pretenses. "I'm here because of your daughter, Mrs. Brawney."

The woman winced as if she'd been slapped hard in the face. "She's not… I mean."

"Oh, no, nothing like that," Hannah said, quickly realizing Olivia's mother had assumed the worst. "Olivia's alive and well. She lives in Seattle and is one of the best-known interior designers in the city."

The woman put her hand to her chest and exhaled slowly. "That girl," she said, her voice cracking with emotion. "I knew Olivia Faye would be somebody. She was so set on breaking out of this life."

"Tell me about her," Hannah said. "What was she like as a girl?"

"She was a prissy thing, and what an imagination. Always pretending to be a princess in a fairy tale, twirling around like Cinderella at the ball. I didn't have any extra money to buy her nice things, but every now and then some of the women from the church would bring over a box of clothes they didn't want no more, and Olivia Faye would dig through them like they was treasure."

"Was she a good student?"

"She was smart, but she didn't like school—said

they made fun of the way she dressed. She came home crying about that all the time. I wasn't surprised a bit when she quit school at sixteen and came to work with me at the Supermart. Not that she worked much. She used to sneak over to the magazine rack and spend hours staring at those fancy-dressed movie stars.

"I used to tell her to quit dreaming and get to work, but she never paid me no mind. She just saved every penny she got her hands on and told me she was going to be living in some fancy house with a pool one day, wearing those slinky designer gowns and expensive jewelry, and riding around in a big car."

"Well, she did it, Mrs. Brawney," Hannah said. "She got all that and more. How long has it been since you've seen her?"

"Let's see." She thought for a minute. "It's been forty-five years."

"You mean, she's never been back to visit you since she left at twenty-one?"

"No. She's got a full life. Besides, I'd just embarrass her. You can look at me and see I don't have any money, just that check social security sends me."

"Did she go to Smith College?" Jack asked.

"Smith College? Where's that?"

"In Massachusetts. It's a very prestigious women's college."

Dorothy shook her head. "I don't see how she could have. She didn't even finish high school."

Hannah tried to mesh the two images of her mother—the sophisticated but headstrong woman who'd raised her and the determined dreamer from Mendos Supermart. It wasn't nearly as difficult a task as she would have imagined. But other issues were harder to accept. ''Have you heard from Olivia at all?''

''She used to write sometimes—told me when she got married and that she'd had a daughter. I asked her to bring my granddaughter to see me. She said she would, but she never did. That's Olivia Faye for you. She's not much on keeping in touch.''

Hannah nodded. ''You must miss her terribly.''

''A mother always misses her child, but you can't hold on to them no more than you can hold on to one of those bubbles the kids blow. You try, and they burst. Either way, you lose them. I'm just glad to hear she's doing well and is happy. She is happy, isn't she?''

''Most likely,'' Hannah said. And if she wasn't, she'd be busy finding a way to get what she needed to make her happy.

''I go to morning mass every day, and I always say a prayer for Olivia Faye. I light a candle for her, too. I don't ask that she come home, even though I sure would like to see her. All I ever ask is that my little girl is safe.''

If Olivia had picked up anything from her mother, it was her faith, Hannah decided, though she couldn't imagine that her mother's prayers had ever been that unselfish.

''I still don't understand why you're here,'' Dorothy said, looking from Hannah to Jack. ''Are you writing a magazine article about Olivia Faye? She'd love being in one of those magazines she was always looking at, but I doubt she'd want anything about me in it.''

''No,'' Jack said. ''That's not why we're here.'' He put an arm around Hannah's shoulders. She turned to meet his gaze and knew he was thinking it was time for her to tell her grandmother who she really was.

Hannah trembled, then turned to Dorothy. "I'm here because Olivia is my mother."

The older woman gasped. "What did you say?"

"Your daughter is my mother. I came here because I wanted to know more about her past."

Dorothy stared at her own clasped hands for long seconds before she looked up and faced Hannah. When she did, tears moistened her dark brown eyes. "You're Olivia's daughter?"

"Yes."

"You're my granddaughter? You're Hannah?"

Finally the emotions hit, though Hannah couldn't have named the feelings that tugged at her heart and tightened her chest. "I am, and I'm sorry we've had to wait this long to meet."

Tears rolled down the woman's sallow cheeks. She rummaged a tissue from her pocket and dabbed at her eyes. "You're so pretty. Prettier even than my Olivia Faye was."

The room grew quiet. A multitude of secrets stood between the two women, but fate and blood bound them together. "I'm sorry we never knew each other, but we can start now," Hannah said, "unless you'd rather just let the past stay dead."

"Oh, sweetie. You're not the past. And now that you're here, I sure don't want to lose you the way I lost Olivia."

Hannah stood and walked over to her grandmother. "Then I guess you just got a new granddaughter and a great-grandson who's not here." She patted her slightly rounded belly. "And another great-grandchild on the way."

"Father John always said I had a blessing coming to me, but I never expected a godsend like you." She stood and put her arms around Hannah.

Tears gathered in Hannah's eyes. At least now she knew why she'd flown halfway across the country to verify for herself that everything she knew about Olivia's past was a bitter lie. She was the answer to a lonely mother's prayer.

"A LIFETIME BUILT ON LIES and fantasies," Hannah said once she and Jack were back in the car. "I wonder how much of this Dad knows."

"Your father's a smart man. He probably knows a lot more about your mother than you think. I wouldn't be surprised if he knows about her affair with Louis or that you're not his biological daughter."

"Maybe, but I'll never be the one to tell him that. He is my father in every way that counts."

"I think you should talk to your mother before you say anything to him or anyone else about what you learned today."

"Why bother talking to her? I'd only get more lies."

"Maybe not. People change, Hannah. Look how I changed over the years."

Indeed he had. From bad boy to terrific father and husband, not that he didn't still have a few bad boy tricks for the bedroom. But this wasn't about the kind of irresponsibility and immaturity Jack had exhibited. "You never lied about who and what you were, Jack. Not the way Mother has."

"I'm not saying you should condone her behavior, just give her a chance to explain."

"I'll try, but it would be a lot easier if I didn't know she'd thrown her own mother away." She leaned back and closed her eyes, blocking out the glaring rays of the sun, but only bringing the doubts that plagued her into keener focus. And front and center, shadowing all the disturbing truths she'd discovered about her mother the last few days, was an antique crystal cross.

FATHER DOM LOBIANCO took the carton of milk from the refrigerator, poured himself a tall glass of it and got a couple of cookies from the pantry. Though he was physically tired, he couldn't sleep, and he hated lying in bed and staring at the ceiling. Better to move around and try to clear his mind. When a man was nearing seventy-one, as Dom was, there were always a few nights a year when sleep escaped you.

Cookies and milk in hand, he walked to the back door and stared out at the moonlit gardens and low brick wall that separated the rectory from the chapel. The shadow of the cross fell over the stone path. The sight of it usually soothed him, but tonight it only reminded him of the cross he had turned over to the Seattle police.

Such a history, that piece. Stolen from Our Lady of Mercy the night Father Michael Cleary was killed, only to be returned twenty-one years later by a young woman a few hours before her death. He hadn't known Michael well, but he had met him several times.

Father Michael was a popular priest who loved church history, especially as it related to religious icons. He was the one who'd first identified the crystal cross as an important relic, and he'd been storing it at Our Lady of Mercy until it could be professionally evaluated. It was so sad that the cross might have cost him his life.

But the murder case was in the hands of the police again, and maybe this time they'd be more successful. Dom had made certain the new generation of cops knew the full story.

According to another priest who had actually been with Michael that night, Michael had received a call about two in the morning from one of his parishioners. He'd seemed upset, and about a half hour after the call he'd said he was going out for a walk. The priest had tried to get him to stay in, considering the hour, but Michael had gone anyway. The next morning his body had been found inside the church, and the crystal cross was missing.

The police had surmised that the attacker was a druggie looking for cash. He'd probably seen Michael leave and had been waiting when the young priest returned.

As far as Dom was concerned, the theory had more holes in it than his robe the year the moths nested inside it. For one thing, too few people knew about the cross, which made it very unlikely that a common crook would know of its existence much less its value. Second, the only other thing taken had been the cash out of Michael's pockets, even though there had been other valuable icons left untouched. And third, there was no sign of a struggle.

Dom thought it far more likely that the killer had been a friend or perhaps a desperate parishioner who knew that the cross was on site.

Killed by a friend. It was a sad thought, indeed.

BEN STOOD at the door to his son's room, watching him sleep. Doug would celebrate his third birthday tomorrow, albeit six months late. It would be a momentous occasion, with cake, ice cream, friends and ponies. His son had helped make the invitations, picked out the cake design and chosen the plates and napkins at the party store in the mall. He was growing up.

It seemed just yesterday that Ben had rushed Vicki to the hospital. He hadn't been the doctor in charge of the delivery, of course, but he'd been right there, seen his son's tiny head when he'd pushed out of the birth canal. He still remembered that first cry. And the way Vicki had looked when he'd put their newborn son in her arms.

Less than two years later he'd watched her die.

Pulling the door shut, Ben walked down the stairs and to the back door. A light mist was falling and layers of clouds hid the stars and moon. Still, he opened the door and stepped into the cool dampness of the night. His bare feet slapped the grass as he made his way to the foot of the maple tree that grew next to Doug's swing set.

Ben had planted the tree at Vicki's request. She'd wanted some visual reminder for Ben that her spirit was always watching over him. But it had been symbolic for Ben, as well, a way of holding on to a remnant of the kind of love he'd never expected to find again.

Ben dropped into Doug's swing and stretched out his feet so the swing could sway gently as thoughts and feelings from the past merged with the present. "We did well, Vicki," he whispered. "We have a beautiful and wonderful son. He's like you in so many ways. He has your smile and your eyes, and your gentleness. He's the light of my life, but I need more."

He hesitated, half afraid guilt would swell inside him, but all he felt was a cool breeze that tousled his hair and prickled his flesh. He got out of the swing and leaned against the trunk of the tree. The vow Vicki had extracted from him before her death echoed in his mind.

She'd made him promise that he wouldn't let grief destroy him, but that he'd honor her love by being the best doctor he could be, by working to provide child care on the hospital site, and mostly by just going on with his life. She'd assured him that she not only expected but wanted him to love again. At the time, he'd thought he never could.

But now there was Alexandra. He couldn't explain his feelings for her. They'd come on too fast and too strong. But they were there inside him, creating a need so powerful that it physically hurt to go a whole day without seeing her.

Their relationship was so different from what his and Vicki's had been. With Vicki, the attraction had grown slowly, the feelings had been less intense, more sane. With Alexandra, the sparks had been instant, though he'd tried hard to hide them. The relationship was still new, but already traumatic—a whirlwind of nightmares and fright, and of passion that raged out of control.

He couldn't get her out of his mind for a second. He needed her even when she was pushing him away, ached for her when she was threatening to run. And when he'd made love with her, it had been as if heaven and earth had exploded inside him.

But if he brought her into his life—into Doug's life—would they wake up one day to find that she'd simply packed her bags and run away? Would they be forced to face excruciating grief a second time?

It wouldn't matter for him. Losing Alexandra now would be just as heartbreaking as losing her later. But what would it do to Doug?

"Give me a sign, Vicki. Let me know what to do."

But the only sign was that the mist turned to rain and soaked through his pajamas as he slowly made his way back to the house.

ALEXANDRA SLEPT LATE on Saturday morning, grateful that she'd finally had a night free of terrifying dreams, the first since the hypnosis session. Her next appointment was on Monday afternoon. She hoped she'd find answers and not just more of the twisted nightmares that had followed the last session.

She hadn't seen or heard from Gary since the night he'd brought her the doll, but she was going back into the underground tunnels today to search for him. And she hadn't had any more unwanted visitors or candle deliveries, probably because Ben had hired off-duty cops to stand guard outside her apartment every night.

Her thoughts turned to Ben. Actually she never went long without thinking of him, without reliving every glorious moment of their lovemaking. Tender and sweet. Wanton and passionate. He was everything a woman could want. She knew she was falling in love with him, if she wasn't there already.

But loving him didn't make the nightmares vanish or the terror disappear. And loving him wouldn't guarantee a happy-ever-after. She knew that even if Ben didn't.

He and Doug would be getting ready for this afternoon's birthday party. Doug had begged her to come again yesterday, and it had been difficult to tell him no when he'd looked at her with those big, brown, pleading eyes. But she couldn't possibly go to that house. Just thinking about it sent chilling tremors shooting up her spine.

Still she should call and tell him she hoped he had a great time at his belated birthday celebration. She picked up the bedroom phone and punched in the number, expecting Ben to answer. But it was Doug's high-pitched voice that said hello.

"Good morning, Doug."

"Hi, Alexandra."

"I guess you're very excited about the party."

"We can't have a party. We have to call it off." His voice wavered and she could tell he was on the verge of tears.

"What's wrong?"

"Daddy's sick. He's throwing up."

"Is Mrs. Harold there with you?"

"No, she's gone away. We're not going to have cake or games, and the ponies can't come."

Anxiety pushed along Alexandra's every nerve ending. Ben was sick and he needed her. If she needed him, he'd come running. But this was different. She couldn't go to that house. She'd told him all along she couldn't be counted on. He'd believe her now.

But her mind conjured up the image of Ben, pale and nauseous and trying to take care of a very disappointed preschooler. And poor Doug. He'd been so excited about his party this week that he could barely talk of anything else.

She took a deep breath, knowing what she had to do, just not how she could do it. ''Go and tell your daddy I'm on my way over there, Doug. And don't call off your party. I'll help.''

He squealed in delight. ''Daddy! We can have the party.''

A second later Ben was on the phone. ''You don't have to do this, Alexandra.''

''I wouldn't try telling that to Doug if I were you.''

''You're right, not now anyway. Come on over if you're sure.''

''I'm not sure, but I'll be there.''

She was shaking when she broke the connection. In less than an hour she'd be walking up the steps and knocking on the door of the house at Forrester Square East. She had no choice. It was what she had to do.

Heaven help them all.

CHAPTER FOURTEEN

ALEXANDRA STEPPED OUT of the taxi and stared at the house at Forrester Square East. The memories began taking shape as if on cue, but the downward emotional spiral was interrupted by Doug's excited voice. When she looked up, he was running towards her wearing nothing but a pair of blue shorts and one sock.

"You found us!" He bounded down the walk and threw his arms around her. "I thought you were lost."

"No way!"

"Yeah! Now we can have the party."

"Absolutely. But first we better get you dressed."

"I have a Woody cake, and it's just like *Toy Story* with a horse and a cowboy hat and everything. And I have a Woody costume to wear, but I looked in the closet and I can't see it."

"I'll bet the two of us can find it."

"I sure hope so." Doug half ran, half jumped the last few steps up the walk. Alexandra followed him though the large mahogany door. The banister along the winding stairway was of the same dark wood as in her nightmares. Her breath caught, and for one terrifying second she felt the heat of the fire. But then Ben walked in and claimed all her attention.

"You look terrible," she said.

"And I feel so great."

He was in pajama bottoms, topped by a plaid robe that was open and hanging off his shoulders. His feet were bare, his hair disheveled, his face unshaven.

"How long have you been sick?"

"It hit about eight this morning, but I kept hoping it was something I ate."

"Are you throwing up?"

"Only every five minutes or so. The rest of the time I'm lying around hoping to die."

"Should I call a doctor? I mean, another doctor. One who specializes in stomach problems."

"No. I had a dozen or more patients in the office this past week with a twenty-four-hour gastrointestinal virus. I usually avoid those irksome plagues, but this time I wasn't so lucky. I'm taking something for nausea. There's nothing else to do."

"What about fluids? You don't want to dehydrate."

"You should be a doctor. You sound just like one."

"I'd never stay in one place long enough to get the degree." She regretted the words before they were out of her mouth. What she'd said was true, but it wasn't what Ben wanted to hear, and she didn't want to get into that now.

"Are you running a fever?" she asked before he had a chance to challenge her previous comment. She stepped towards him to put a hand to his forehead, but he backed away.

"No fever, but don't touch, and don't come any closer. Believe me, you don't want to catch this bug."

"You're right. So go back to bed. Doug and I will handle the party."

"Are you certain you want to do this? If I can get

you to call the people on the guest list, we can postpone until next week. I probably can't get the ponies then, but everything else would work.''

''Daddy,'' Doug protested. ''We have to have the ponies. I told my friends.''

''Yeah, Daddy,'' Alexandra mimicked. ''What's a birthday party without ponies?''

''There's going to be a dozen or more preschoolers on the back lawn,'' he said, giving her another chance to back out. ''It may be a party, but it won't be a picnic.''

''I work at a day care, remember? Kids are my specialty.'' Doug grinned and scooted close to her, obviously pleased she was not being swayed to the opposition. She put her hands on his shoulders. ''What do you think, Doug? Can we handle this?''

He beamed. ''We can do it easy!''

Ben shrugged, but she could tell from the way he looked at her that he was both pleased and relieved.

''I won't be any help. I'll have to stay upstairs and far away from the guests, but I think everything's ready. The party favors are in the kitchen and the...'' Ben stopped talking and turned a deeper shade of green.

''It's under control, Ben. Go back to bed, before I have to carry you back.''

This time he only nodded, then ducked into the nearest bathroom. Poor guy. But if his diagnosis was right, he should be feeling better in another twenty hours or so. She took Doug by the hand. ''Let's go find that Woody costume. We're having a birthday party.''

''This is going to be *stupendous.*''

''Stupendous,'' she agreed, unless the house

freaked her out and she treated the birthday guests to Nightmare on Forrester Square. No. Better not to even let that idea skitter across her brain. She absolutely could not let that happen.

ALEXANDRA BREATHED A SIGH of relief as the last party guest was loaded into his car seat and his mother backed out of the Jessups's driveway. As Ben had predicted, it had not been a picnic, but it hadn't been all that bad, either, unless you were offended by pony poop. Fortunately, she had a strong stomach for that sort of thing.

The back lawn where the party was held was more like a park than a yard. There was an area of gardens with benches, statues and a gazebo, a play area for Doug with an elaborate wooden swing set and a fort, and a cleared area big enough for a game of badminton, croquet or touch football. Only today, that was where the pony rides had taken place.

Doug and his guests had a terrific time. How could they not, with ponies to ride. And not just pony rides. Ben had arranged for one of the local trainers to come out to tell them all about horses—what they ate, what type of care they needed, how fast they could run—all at a level the children could appreciate.

They'd eaten their cake and ice cream on a couple of plastic picnic tables that had been set up under a large shade tree near the gardens. After they were thoroughly smeared in cake frosting and crumbs, Alexandra had kept the young guests entertained with active games and a story she'd made up on the spot about a pony whose only wish was for a little boy to love.

But now the party was over and she was ready for

a drink of something stronger than fruit juice and a nice easy chair to sink into. Doug, however, was bouncing off the walls from an overdose of excitement and sugar. She settled him in the living room floor with one of his new toys and went upstairs to check on the patient, who'd been on his own since the party had started.

She walked to the door at the end of the hall, then stopped, suddenly swamped with memories. The house was laid out almost exactly the way she remembered her own home. The room her parents had shared had been here, just off the stairs.

Memories rushed her mind as she leaned against the wall. Running into her parents' room and crawling into bed with them when it thundered. She and her father cooking breakfast for her mother and serving it to her in bed. Her mother…

No. She couldn't let the memories take over. It was too risky when she had Doug to care for. But if these images were still stored in her memory bank, there could be any number of significant details there, as well—repressed for twenty-one years, just as Dr. Abrams had said.

The door to the master suite was closed. She knocked gently and tried to sound nonchalant. "Are you still alive and kicking in there?"

"Alive, but I feel more like I've been kicked by those ponies I heard neighing outside."

She eased the door open. Ben looked a little more alert, but tired. Even in this state, he was practically irresistible.

"Just thought you'd like an update," she said, moving in a little closer but keeping a good distance between them. "The last guest has departed, and the party was a *stupendous* success."

"Did Doug have a good time?"

"He had a blast. I'm sorry you weren't there to see it."

"Me, too. I looked forward to the party with fear and trembling, but I still hate that I missed it."

"I took pictures with the camera that was on the table."

"Great."

"Are you feeling any better?"

"A little. Pretty weak, but my stomach has calmed."

"How about some soup and crackers? That should go easy on your system."

"Sounds good," he said, rising up on his elbows. "But you've done more than enough today."

"How much trouble can it be to open and heat a can of soup?"

"Sounds monumental to me right now."

"Which is why I'll do it for you. Just stay in bed and I'll bring it up as soon as it's ready."

"I'll come downstairs. I have to anyway before you leave so I can keep an eye on Doug."

"You're in no shape for that. I'll get Doug a light supper and a bath, then stay with him until he falls asleep. As active as he's been today, that probably won't take long."

"And you're okay with that?"

She knew what he meant. Was she okay in this house where the demons who tormented her had all been born? "So far," she answered. "Perhaps even ghosts are daunted by ponies and excited children."

"Or maybe it's a sign that..."

She shook her head. ''Don't read anything into today, Ben. You and Doug needed me, and I came, but nothing's changed.''

The silence grew strained between them.

''You could spend the night, Alexandra.''

''You are too sick to stand up. Don't tell me you're thinking about playing around.''

''I'm a man. We're always thinking about it. But that's all I could handle tonight, even if this virus weren't contagious. But there are three empty guest rooms.''

''I've made it though the day because I haven't had time to think. I'm not pushing my luck by sleeping over.''

''You're going to hypnotherapy to try and release trapped memories. Staying here might produce the same effect.''

''And have me screaming and scaring Doug half to death.''

''He's had nightmares before. He'd understand when we explain it to him.''

''Not going to happen, Ben. By the time it's dark, I plan to be back in my own apartment. Now, back to the soup. I checked earlier. There's chicken noodle, beef vegetable and cream of potato in the pantry. Do you have a preference?''

''Chicken noodle. I could get used to this, you know.''

''Soup?''

''Served by you. Or serving it to you. I'm a new millennium kind of guy.''

''Save the charm. I'm not coming near those germs.''

"Then better just drop the soup off at the door when you bring it up."

"You got it, Doc." She'd gladly comply with that request. Being with Ben frightened her much more than the virus. If she wasn't careful, she might begin to believe they could have a future together, that she could live in this house and in his world on a permanent basis. That the past could be sorted out and tucked away in a neat little compartment the way it worked with most people.

She might believe for a while, but then the nightmare would show up and prove her wrong.

ALEXANDRA CHECKED IN on Doug one last time. He was sprawled across the bed, one foot and leg under the sheet, the other foot and leg on top. His stuffed lion was tucked under one arm and one of the action figures he'd gotten for his birthday was clutched tightly in his right hand. She tiptoed over and kissed him on the cheek, lightly so as not to wake him.

The house was quiet as she gathered her things and started down the wide staircase. She'd already said good-night to Ben and told him she'd let herself out. He'd actually improved to the point that he'd showered and shaved and asked for a second bowl of soup.

All was well. Time for her to go. She lingered for a second outside Doug's door, but the second was all it took for the next wave of memories to attack.

Doug's door. But her room had been upstairs, as well, very near this same spot. The walls had been a pale green, her bed a four-poster, white, with a soft pink awning over it. The Barbie dollhouse her father had built for her occupied one corner. She and Hannah and Katherine had played with their dolls there.

She'd had a little car for hers to ride in. Katherine had a pony for hers.

The memories tumbled inside her, fragments with no connecting ties, as if they'd been shaken in a box, then dumped to fall at will. Tugging the well-chewed rubber ball from Mr. Wiggles's mouth; making cookies with her mother; catching a ride down the steps on her father's shoulders.

Her mother's voice, loud and angry. "You will not ruin my life, Jonathan Webber. I've worked too hard to get where I am."

"Don't be foolish. Put the gun away."

Alexandra was on the landing now. She could see the gun and the candle and the flame. The grandfather clock started to sound the hour. One. Two. Three.

"No. No. Oh, please, no!"

But the bullet cracked like thunder. Mary Jane slipped through Alexandra's fingers. Father Michael crashed into the candle, blood spurting from his shoulder like a fountain. The flames started licking their way along Mommy's sofa and spread to the long silky drapes. Smoke rolled up like black clouds, and Alexandra's little legs were getting hot beneath her nightgown.

"Daddy? Help me, Daddy. Daaaddy!"

BEN JUMPED FROM THE BED the second he heard Alexandra's scream. Not bothering to grab a robe, he raced down the steps in his pajamas and gathered her in his arms. "It's okay, baby. I have you. You're okay."

She flailed for a few minutes the way she had the other night, but this time she quieted more quickly.

When she looked up at him, her eyes were wide with terror.

"I know how he died."

"What are you talking about?"

"Father Michael Cleary. I know how he died. My mother shot him."

"Your mother couldn't have killed Father Michael. He was shot in Our Lady of Mercy church."

"No. I saw it as clear as day."

"You were only six years old. How can you remember what Michael Cleary looked like?"

"He's in one of the pictures I got from Katherine. He looked exactly the same in the memories that took over my mind."

Her words chilled him. He'd been certain she was dealing with repressed memories. But the account she gave now was more like a tortured hallucination.

"I think you should talk to Dr. Abrams about this before you tell anyone else, Alexandra."

"So in case I'm going mad, no one will know but the two of us and my shrink."

"So he can help you sort out the memories and separate nightmare from fact."

She pulled away from him. "I need to go, Ben."

"Stay here with Doug and me tonight."

"You don't need a haunted lunatic screwing up your life."

"I don't need a lunatic, but I do need you."

"So I can ruin your life and Doug's with my nightmares and flights into horror land? So I can wake you at night with bloodcurdling screams?" Exasperation made her voice crack like a leather whip. "I'm not even fit to work at your satellite center. So tell me,

Ben, exactly what is it about me that you need in your life?"

Ben met her fiery gaze. Last night he'd asked for a sign, a way to know if loving Alexandra would be right for him and his son. Or maybe he'd been asking Vicki for some kind of release, though she'd given that before she died. The funny thing was, he didn't need a sign anymore.

"I want all of you, Alexandra. I love you and I can't imagine not having you in my life. Doug loves you, too. You don't have to be perfect to earn our love. We just love you because we do."

"Don't do this to me, Ben. Please, don't do this to me."

"If you're asking me not to love you, you may as well ask me to learn to fly or to walk on the moon."

Tears glistened in her eyes. She was hurting, but he couldn't let up on her. Not now. She had to stay and fight—for herself. For him. And even for Doug. "I never expected to find love like this twice in my life—never thought it possible. I lost the first woman I loved to a disease, but I will not lose you to a nightmare."

"Oh, Ben. What have we done?"

"Fallen in love. And that can't be wrong."

"You'd think, wouldn't you? But it is."

"Stay here tonight. Give us a chance."

"You ask so much."

"We have so much to gain."

"I can't promise forever, Ben."

"No one can. All anyone has is right now." He took her hand and they climbed the stairs together. She hadn't told him she loved him back. He could live with that, though it would have meant the world to him if she had said the words. But she'd been through so much, and still had battles to fight. He would wait as long as it took.

He could handle anything but losing her.

GARY WAS DIRTY, tattered and years older than he'd been the last time Ernie had seen him. It had taken the retired agent a long time to locate him, but once he had, he knew in an instant that he was standing in front of the man whose life he'd helped destroy. "Hi, Gary. Long time, no see."

Gary squinted and stared. "Have you got any money to spare?"

"Yeah. Why don't I buy you some dinner? How about a hamburger?"

"How about a steak?"

"A steak sounds good." But not the kind they'd get at any dive that would let Gary in. "Tell you what. Come back to my hotel with me, and I'll order a steak from the room service menu."

"I can't go."

"I'll bring you back."

"No. I've got to stay here. Will you buy me a steak?"

"Sure, if you'll sit down and talk to me while you eat it."

"Talk about what?"

"I'd like to talk about you. And me. My name is Ernie Brooks. Do you remember me? FBI? Eagle Aerotech? Louis Kinard? Jonathan Webber?"

Gary stopped shuffling his feet and looked right into Ernie's eyes. The stare was no longer glazed but stony. "What are you doing here, Ernie?"

"I came to see you."

"I did what you said. Now leave me alone."

"I'm not here to cause trouble. I want to help."

Gary slumped against the side of the building, far back in the alley where Ernie had found him. His eyes took on that vacant look again and he stared past Ernie to watch a tom cat that had jumped up on a trash can a few feet from them. "Have you got some money to spare, mister?"

The confusion had taken hold again, but Gary had seemed lucid for a few moments, which meant there could be times when he remembered everything. Those fragments of memory must have lured him back to Seattle.

Which meant Ernie no longer had a choice. Rules be damned. In the end, a man always did what he had to do.

ALEXANDRA WAS IN the office a half hour before the first children were due to arrive on Monday morning so that she could make certain everything was in order for the new week. Hannah wouldn't be in until afternoon since her plane landed at eleven-thirty. She hadn't volunteered any reason for her sudden decision to take this trip and hadn't disclosed her destination. She'd just left Adam with her father and taken off. Spontaneous trips like that weren't like Hannah, but then the idea might have been Jack's. A chance to have his wife all to himself.

Alexandra returned a couple of phone calls to parents who'd left messages over the weekend inquiring about the day-care program. By the time she finished, the first child had arrived. She took a walk through the building and spotted Doug hanging his blue windbreaker on a peg. When he finished, he bent over and picked up a small stuffed animal.

"Hi, there, Doug."

"Hi."

He turned so that she got a good look at his stuffed animal. A white shar-pei puppy. Her heart jumped to her throat and her mind flashed the memory of Mr. Wiggles prancing about and getting tangled in her feet.

"Where did you get the dog, Doug?"

"From you. Don't you remember?"

"I didn't give you that."

"You left it for me. It was all wrapped in silvery paper."

"No, there's some mistake."

"Daddy said it was from you. He told me to say thank-you."

Alexandra stood silently, forcing herself to stay calm. She might slide in and out of reality, but she would never have bought a stuffed shar-pei for anyone, let alone have sent it to the place where Mr. Wiggles had burned to death.

She walked back to the office and dialed Ben's cellular phone number. Hoping for a miracle, knowing there wouldn't be one.

ALEXANDRA WAS SHAKING by the time she hung up the phone. The gift had been in the front seat of Ben's car when he'd left for work that morning. He'd thought it odd, but had just assumed she'd picked up something after she'd left Sunday afternoon and dropped it off during the few minutes he and Doug had walked over to the park. The note had simply said, "Happy birthday. Love, Alexandra."

This weekend she'd had a glimmer of hope. Now even that was dashed by an act of unspeakable cruelty. But why? That was the question that hammered in her mind as she stood and stared out the window looking out on Sandringham Drive. Why would anyone drag an innocent child into a sordid game of threats and terror?

Alexandra was still staring out the window when the phone rang. She knew something was seriously wrong the second Griffin said her name.

CHAPTER FIFTEEN

ALEXANDRA'S GRASP tightened on the receiver. "What now?" she asked, dreading Griffin's answer.

"Gary Devlin is in Seattle Memorial Hospital."

"Oh, no." She sank to the nearest chair. "What's wrong? Is it his heart?"

"He was beaten with a blunt object about the head and body."

"How bad is it?"

"The doctor described his condition as guarded. He'd have probably been dead if a guy who worked at one of the restaurants hadn't gone out the back door to dump his trash when he did. He yelled and frightened off the attacker."

"Can I see him?"

"Probably, but I don't recommend it. He's bruised and swollen so bad he barely looks human. No use to put yourself through that when he won't know you're there."

"He'd know someone was with him."

"Not now. He was dazed and out of his head when the ambulance picked him up, but he slipped into a coma shortly after arriving at the hospital."

Alexandra's insides twisted into ragged knots. "Do you have any idea who did this, or why?"

"Not a clue. The man who stopped the attack said the other guy appeared to be part of the homeless population, but I have my doubts. It was far too brutal. Those guys might squabble over a cardboard box or throw a few fists over two drops of booze left in a whiskey bottle, but they don't go in for the kill."

"He didn't deserve it," Alexandra said.

"Maybe."

"What's that supposed to mean?"

"Just that there are lots of unanswered questions about Devlin. The man had a past, and pasts have a way of catching up with you."

"His hadn't, not until I sent his fingerprints in to be checked."

"Don't go thinking this is your fault, Alexandra."

Only she did think that. The same way Doug's getting the shar-pei puppy was her fault. Everything she touched turned tragic.

She thanked Griffin for calling, hung up the phone, then forced her body to action. She had a few things to do, and then she was out of here. To the hospital to check on Gary. Home to pack a few clothes. And then a taxi to the airport. She had to get out of town while everyone she knew and loved was still alive.

She ached to call Ben, just to hear his voice when he said her name. But she'd never been able to handle goodbyes. Already it felt as if her heart were splitting in two. She should have never let him into her life. Never learned to care the way she did.

But how could she not love Ben?

HANNAH HAD THREE messages waiting when her plane landed in Seattle. One from her mother, one from her father and one from Alexandra. She dialed her mother's cell phone number while they waited for their luggage at baggage claim.

They'd barely said hello when her mother got down to the reason for her call. "I think you need to go straight to Seattle Memorial Hospital and check on Alexandra."

"Is she ill?"

"No, but that homeless man she's so obsessed with was attacked and beaten last night. He's half dead and in a coma. Needless to say, Alexandra rushed up there to be with him. It's not healthy. No wonder she freaks out so often."

"Slow down, Mother, and stick to the facts."

This time Olivia explained the situation in slightly more detail. Griffin Frazier had called her in an attempt to track down Hannah, because he thought Alexandra needed someone with her at the hospital. Hannah agreed.

"Thanks for letting me know, Mother. I was going straight to the day care, but I'll make a stop at the hospital first."

"Good. Call me when you get there and let me know how she's doing. I've been so worried about her ever since you told me about her nightmares. The best thing that can happen to Alexandra is for that man to die. Then maybe she'd leave Seattle and her dreadful past behind once and for all."

"I don't agree. I think it's time she faced the past and dealt with it."

"That might be true for some people, but not for Alexandra. Seattle holds nothing but heartache for her."

"That can change."

"Oh, Hannah. I'm not sure how I raised a daughter as naive as you."

"Probably because you never let me know the real

you, Mother." She couldn't keep the sting from her tone.

"Well, right now my concern is for Alexandra, and yours should be, as well."

"I have faith in her ability to work through this." Hannah didn't bother to argue the fact. No one had ever changed her mother's opinion on anything, and this time it didn't really matter. But there were other issues that did matter. "I need to talk you, Mother."

"We are talking, dear."

"I need to talk to you in person."

"I have appointments all day, and Drake and I have dinner plans for this evening. Perhaps later in the week."

"Cancel your dinner plans. I need to talk to you *tonight.*"

"What is this about?"

"It's about Olivia Faye Brawney from New Mexico, and about an antique crystal cross."

The silence seemed to go on forever, but when Olivia spoke, her voice was steady and controlled. "I'll get back to you later, Hannah. I have urgent business to take care of now."

She broke the connection without giving Hannah a chance to respond. So like Olivia to have the last word. But she wouldn't be able to cut Hannah off so easily tonight.

OLIVIA GUNNED the accelerator and went sailing past the traffic light just as it turned from yellow to red. Her insides were pitching and turning, her pulse racing.

Things were spinning out of control, as fast as they'd spun twenty-one years ago when Jonathan

Webber had turned on all of them. No matter how well she planned or how hard she worked, someone was ready to step in and spoil it for her. Life wasn't fair. But then she'd learned that long ago when she'd had nothing while other girls in her school had it all.

Olivia swerved onto a side street. She had a very busy day ahead of her, but first she'd stop at Our Lady of Mercy and ask forgiveness. Without it, there was no peace.

HANNAH TOOK THE HOSPITAL elevator to the eleventh floor, then followed the signs to Room 1188. Alexandra was there, sitting in a chair pulled next to the bed where Gary Devlin was hooked up to an IV and oxygen. Hannah didn't say a word, just crossed the floor and gave her friend a hug.

"Thanks for coming," Alexandra said.

"I'm glad I could." She looked down at Gary Devlin. "Is he still in a coma?"

"Yes. I've tried to talk to him, but there's no response."

"Do they know who did this to him?"

"No, but I can't help thinking I'm responsible. Everything I touch meets with disaster."

"Oh, sweetie. This isn't your fault. The course of this man's life was set long before you met him."

"I don't think so, Hannah."

Hannah could see the pain in Alexandra's eyes. Maybe Olivia was right this time. Perhaps leaving the city would be the only thing that could save Alexandra from her memories and from herself.

A short while later Hannah hugged her friend goodbye and left. Alexandra didn't even seem to notice.

GARY BLINKED, then opened his eyes. Alexandra jumped to attention, bending over him so that she could hear anything he murmured. "It's Alexandra, Gary. You're at the hospital and you're all right."

He turned towards the sound of her voice. "Kitten?"

Her heart leaped. "Yes. It's Kitten." She took his hand. "I'm here."

"You're going to be all right, Kitten."

"So are you, Daddy. So are you."

"I have to go away, and I won't be coming back. Do what your mother says and always remember that I love you."

"I did, Daddy. I always remembered that." Tears burned at the backs of her eyelids, but a gentle warmth filled her. It was as if her father had reached through the years and taken her in his arms again.

"Who hurt you?" she asked. "Who attacked you?" She waited for an answer, but he'd closed his eyes and turned away. "Talk to me, Daddy. Please talk to me."

If he heard her at all, he gave no sign. But he'd been with her for a second. And as crazy as it seemed, this really was her father. After all these years, he'd come back. But back from where? She wouldn't question that now. He was alive. And he was here.

Tears were streaming down her face as she went to get the nurse. Someone should know that he'd come to for a few precious seconds. She glanced at her watch.

It was five minutes past the time for her appointment with Dr. Abrams. She hadn't planned to keep it after Doug had walked in with the stuffed shar-pei, but she'd give Dr. Abrams and the hypnosis one more chance. For herself, for Ben and Doug, and for her father. One more chance to find out what really happened on the night of July 19, 1983, twenty-one years ago to the day.

She stopped at the nurses' station just long enough to let them know that the patient had come to and said a few words. Then she ran to the elevator. Dr. Abrams would be waiting.

"YOU AND MARY JANE are on the landing," Dr. Abrams said. "The clock is striking the hour. How many times does it strike?"

"One. Two. Three."

"Now what's happening?"

"Mommy has a gun in her hand. She's going to shoot Daddy." Alexandra's breathing was choppy, her voice youthful and shaky. She clapped her palms over her ears and winced.

"Did your mother pull the trigger?"

"Yes. It was so loud, and… I dropped Mary Jane, and I want her back."

"Is your father hurt?"

"No. Mommy didn't shoot Daddy. She shot Father Michael. He fell across the table. His legs are sticking up in the air and he's all bloody."

"When did Father Michael arrive?"

"He just ran in the door and tried to grab a piece of paper from Daddy."

"What's happening now?"

"The candle fell onto the sofa. Daddy's trying to put out the fire, but he can't. The flames are too big. The whole sofa's on fire and the curtains, too. I see Mary Jane on the floor. I have to get her before she burns up in the fire."

"Are you going downstairs?"

"I'm trying to, but I'm falling, and the fire is so hot. I can't breathe. I can't. And everyone is screaming. Help me, Daddy. Please help me."

"Does your daddy help you?"

"Yes, he's got me in his arms now. We're running for the door."

"Where's your mother?"

"She's on the stairs, right behind us. Daddy's reaching back to grab her hand. We go all the way out to the street, but my face is still hot from the fire. The fire is noisy and flames are shooting out the roof. And Mr. Wiggles is barking." Alexandra buried her head in her hands. "Don't let Mr. Wiggles die. Please don't let him die."

"Are your mother and father still with you?"

"No. Daddy is running back into the house. Mother is screaming at him not to go, but he's going anyway."

Alexandra began to shake and sob uncontrollably. One more minute and he'd have to pull her out. But she was so close now, on the verge of seeing the whole picture and hopefully breaking free of the death grip the past held on her.

"Who's with you now?"

"No one. I'm all alone. Mommy is running back inside the house. I made them both go. I cried for them to save Mr. Wiggles but they couldn't. He's not barking now, but my mother is screaming and screaming."

"But not your daddy?"

"No. No one's screaming now. They're all dead. I killed them. I killed them. I killed them." Alexandra fell over on the couch and rolled up in a fetal position.

The pieces fell into place and Jasper couldn't help but ache for the little girl who'd carried the blame for her parents' death all these years, locked away inside her subconscious. If that weren't enough, she'd watched her mother try to kill her father and end up killing a priest. No wonder she couldn't face the memories.

He released the hypnotic hold, took Alexandra's hands in his and spoke softly as she reentered the present. "You didn't kill anyone, Alexandra. You didn't start the fire, and you didn't make them go back inside. They were the adults. You were just a frightened little girl."

ALEXANDRA WAS NUMB, drained of her energy and most of her emotions as she left Dr. Abrams's office and took the elevator to the crosswalk that led back to the hospital wing. Dr. Abrams had offered to call Ben, but she'd refused. Ben had sick children to take care of, and she needed to be alone. Needed time to work through myriad emotions and sort out the facts that ran wild in her mind.

Had her father really gone back into the burning house for Mr. Wiggles that night? And if her mother hated him so much that she wished him dead, why had she screamed at him not to go and then followed him inside? What horrible things had happened between her parents to make her mother hate her father enough to want to kill him?

But she hadn't killed him. She'd shot Father Michael, the priest they all loved. But Father Michael's body had been found at the church. He'd been killed by the thief who'd stolen the crystal cross.

The pieces didn't fit. Everyone who had anything

to hide should be dead, but if that were so, who had broken into her house and lit dozens of candles to torment her into leaving Seattle? Who had sent the white shar-pei puppy to Doug and signed her name? Who had attacked and tried to kill the homeless man who called her Kitten?

For all the good the hypnosis had done, it had left the most dangerous and terrifying questions unanswered.

The thoughts were whirling in her mind like a carousel gone mad when she reached Room 1188. She walked inside, then stopped. "Olivia, what are you doing here?"

"I was worried about you." She walked over and gave Alexandra a hug. "You've been through so much."

"I appreciate your coming, but I really don't feel like chatting right now. I only stopped by to check on Gary."

"I just talked to the nurse. She says he's unaware of anything that's going on around him now, but they're giving him something for pain."

"That's good." Alexandra stepped to the side of the bed and took his frail hand in hers. It felt so lifeless. But then, so did she.

Olivia stepped up beside her. "I need to talk to you, Alexandra."

"I can't talk now. We'll have to make it another time."

"It's about your parents. I should have told you these things years ago. It might have made a difference in your life."

"What about my parents?"

"I don't want to talk here. Let's take a drive, and

I'll tell you a few more of the deep, dark secrets that the three kings of NorPac and Eagle Aerotech never wanted to reveal.''

It was an offer Alexandra couldn't refuse.

OLIVIA LOOKED FANTASTIC as always. Her perfectly coiffured hair had an auburn tint to it that it hadn't had the last time Alexandra had seen her. But then Olivia was known to change her hair color on a whim. Her slacks were an exquisite linen blend, her blouse a pale yellow silk that looked incredibly expensive, her lips glossy and perfectly defined.

A woman at the top of her form. Alexandra had always found her a little daunting, and it seemed strange that she'd be the one to offer to break what must have been a strictly enforced code of silence regarding company business. But Olivia was more a rule breaker than a rule follower, so maybe it did make sense.

Alexandra was surprised to see a man in the back seat when they approached Olivia's car. ''I thought we'd be alone.''

''We will be, as soon as I drop Drake off at the marina. He's taking the boat out this afternoon.''

''I picked up some coffees,'' Drake said once the introductions were over with and they were on their way. A double chocolate latte with skim foam for you, Alexandra.''

''That's my favorite. How did you know?''

''Olivia told me that you and Hannah were both hooked on them.''

''He remembers everything,'' Olivia said. ''He's a good man to have around.''

''Thanks,'' she said when Drake handed her the

insulated paper cup. She leaned back, sipped her coffee and wondered what information Olivia could possibly have about Carrie and Jonathan Webber that Alexandra didn't already know. Guilt surfaced in suffocating waves at the thought of her parents, the way it had in so many of her nightmares. Then, it had just seemed an undefinable emotion, but now she knew that it had stemmed from her screamed request that they save her puppy. The guilt had fermented inside her, eating away at her until the nightmares relentlessly forced her to face the truth.

It had been too much for her to handle at six. Even now, it was difficult. The fire, the candles, the stuffed shar-pei puppy. They were getting all mixed up, drifting together then parting like dancers trapped in a kaleidoscope.

"How are you feeling, Alexandra?"

She turned to answer Drake, but couldn't bring his face into focus. His features were blurring. "I don't feel well."

"A little dizzy, my dear?" Olivia asked. "Don't worry. Just close your eyes and relax. This will all be over before you know it. You'll be reunited with your parents. Think of this as my favor to you."

Fear engulfed Alexandra. Nothing was clear in her mind except that she was in danger. "Let me out of the car."

"It's too late."

"No." She pushed against the door handle of the speeding car.

"Stop her, Drake!" Olivia screeched.

He yanked Alexandra's hair and she felt the cold nozzle of a pistol at the back of her head.

"I will not let you destroy all I've worked for,"

Olivia said. "No more than I would let your father destroy me."

The words clanged in Alexandra's mind and she could see the red curls bouncing at the back of her mother's head and hear the strained and hateful voice. Only it hadn't been her mother at all. It had been Olivia.

Olivia had…killed…Father…Michael…Cleary.

That was the last thought Alexandra had before she was sucked into swirling darkness.

BEN COULDN'T GET Alexandra off his mind. All Jasper had told him was that there had been a major breakthrough, and though Alexandra was shaken, she'd wanted and needed some time to herself. He'd give her that time, but he had to hear her voice, to know that she was all right.

He went to his office and called her cellular phone number. It rang, but a computerized voice announced that the party he was calling was unavailable. He broke the connection and called the day care. He didn't get Alexandra, but Hannah gave him the news about Gary Devlin. He saw another patient, then turned the last four appointments over to his partner.

It was totally out of character for him to leave before the last patient was dealt with, but emotions he didn't understand were driving him. He had to see Alexandra, and he had to see her now. He rushed to Gary Devlin's hospital room. The panicky feeling mushroomed when he found only a nurse with Gary.

"I'm looking for a friend of Mr. Devlin's. I thought she might be here with him. Her name is Alexandra Webber. Have you seen her?"

The nurse nodded. "I didn't come on duty until

three, but I heard she was here most of the day. She left for a while, but then came back a little after four.''

''How long did she stay?''

''Only a few minutes. I didn't even get a chance to speak to her. Olivia Richards was here and they left together. I wouldn't have recognized Mrs. Richards, but one of the other nurses goes to the same church she does. We were all amazed to have someone as rich and well known as Mrs. Richards visiting one of the homeless who'd been beaten up in a back alley.''

''You're sure they left together?''

''I don't know if they left the hospital together, but they walked out of the patient's room and caught the elevator together. I saw that.''

''Thanks.''

So Alexandra had left with Olivia Richards. But where were they now? He thought of going back to his office and finishing his day, but he was too upset to work. Too upset to think. He was inundated by feelings of desperation, the sense that she was on the run again, that she'd disappear from his life and he'd never be able to find her.

He had never been so afraid.

He tried her cell phone again. When he couldn't get her, he called Hannah. Maybe she'd know something.

ALEXANDRA OPENED her eyes. She tried to move, but her hands and feet were tied and something was stuffed into her mouth. Her mind whirled frantically before her situation came into focus. She was on Olivia's yacht, and it was moving.

She struggled to break free, but only managed to scrape her feet against the wall beside the bed where Olivia and Drake must have placed her. She had no memory of leaving the car or of getting on the boat.

Olivia stuck her head through the door. She was holding a small shiny pistol in her right hand. "Our little Webber princess is getting restless, Drake. Should we give her more of your special coffee?"

"Why bother? She's not going anywhere." He stepped to the side of the bed and yanked the gag from her mouth. "Don't need that anymore. Now that we've left port, there's no one around to hear her if she screams."

Alexandra stared at Olivia. "Why are you doing this to me?"

"Don't try to blame this on me, Alexandra. I didn't want to have to kill you. I tried so very hard not to have to do this. But you wouldn't leave Seattle. You just wouldn't let the past die." She turned to Drake. "Go back and tend the controls. I'll take care of this."

"You killed Father Michael," Alexandra said as Drake walked away.

"Not intentionally. He was one of my best friends. He understood me the way no one else ever had. Even when I confessed my one-night affair with Louis to him, he prayed for my forgiveness."

"You had an affair with Katherine's father? When was this?"

"When Katherine was a baby. Helen had no time for him and he was a handsome and very desirable man. If it hadn't been me, it would have been someone else."

Alexandra sucked in a shaky breath, feeling sick to

her stomach and still dazed from whatever they'd used to put her under. Still, she struggled to make sense of what was going on. "You were the one who sold the software, weren't you?"

"Aren't you the clever one? Not that it will do you any good. You should have heeded my warning, Alexandra. But no, you had to do things your way, just like your stupid, pious father."

"But not so stupid he didn't realize you were guilty."

"Jonathan? He was never so astute. The man honestly believed Louis was guilty."

"That's not true. He knew you were guilty and that's why you were going to kill him."

"All he knew was that I had an affair with Louis. The pompous fool thought he could make me admit it."

The story was sordid—almost too twisted to believe. But Alexandra knew now that Olivia was capable of anything. She also knew that Olivia planned to kill her. Not in a fire, the way her parents had died. No, Olivia intended to shoot her, then bury her in a watery grave. That was the only reason the woman was telling her these things now. That and the fact that Alexandra was the only person she could brag to of her evil deeds without suffering consequences.

Alexandra looked around the cabin, trying to find something that would help her break free if she was left alone again. In the meantime, she had to keep Olivia talking. "How did you get the antique crystal cross? Did you steal it from the church when you took Father Michael's body back?"

"Don't make it sound so terrible. I've given the church far more money over the years than the cross was worth. I've made up for the loss a hundred times over. My only mistake was in hiding the cross in the attic of the beach house and then letting Hannah help me clear away the junk when we remodeled. Actually this is all Hannah's fault. I told her not to touch anything in that part of the attic, but she didn't listen."

"Why did you keep it?"

"It's sacred, and I don't destroy sacred icons."

She couldn't destroy a crystal cross, but she could kill a priest and have an affair with her husband's best friend. It was sick, perverse and twisted.

Olivia stood, straightened her back and her shoulders, and walked out of the room, leaving Alexandra alone again. It would crush Hannah when she learned the things her mother had done—if she learned them. Olivia had fooled them all. And now she was going to kill Alexandra unless she could find some way to stop her.

Alexandra struggled to free her hands as she concentrated on finding a way to escape. Her cellular phone was in her pocket. It had been turned off ever since her appointment with Dr. Abrams, but if she could get to it, hit it with her elbow, she might be able to punch one of her programmed numbers. She doubted it would help. They were probably out of the service area.

But it was worth a try.

BEN GRABBED his cellular phone the second it rang and sucked in a quick breath when his Caller ID said it was Alexandra. "Where are you?"

All he heard was static.

"Where are you, Alexandra? Are you okay?"

He could hear someone's voice, but it was as if the

person was a long way from the phone or on another frequency. Ben strained but couldn't make out what was being said. There was just the distant voice and a familiar humming noise.

"Talk to me, Alexandra. Where are you? Are you with Olivia? Are you in danger? Talk to me." He was screaming now, but she didn't talk to him.

A second later the connection went dead.

THE MINUTES STRETCHED ON as Alexandra waited in the cabin. She had no way of telling the time, but the wait seemed interminable. She was certain they were taking the boat out far enough that her body would likely never be found. Olivia had heard her when she'd tried to use the phone. She'd taken it from her pocket, and that was the last Alexandra had seen of it or Olivia.

Her hands were raw and bloody where she'd struggled against the ropes that bound them. Her head ached, and the rest of her body was growing numb. But her mind kept going, reliving the nightmare and filling in the missing pieces with all she'd learned today.

More than once she'd heard her father's voice saying, *You're all right, Kitten. I have you, and you're all right.* But there was another voice in her head, as well. It was Ben's, saying, *I love you.*

Thoughts and images of Ben flooded her mind. The night he'd made her salad. The way he'd looked running along the beach. The time he'd held her when she was in the throes of the nightmare. The night they'd made love.

The boat shimmied and shook to a stop. A second

later Drake came into the room, picked her up and threw her over his shoulder like a sack of potatoes.

"Guess it's your time, princess. The queen is waiting for you on deck."

"Olivia has killed before, but don't let her make a murderer of you, Drake," Alexandra pleaded. "You can stop her. Take the gun away from her and take us back to the shore."

"No way, sweetheart."

"She doesn't really love you. She's had lots of men. She'll dump you when she's through with you, just like she did the others."

"That's where you're wrong. She won't get a chance to dump me. I'll dump her, but I'll have a nice little bonus check coming in every week. That's how blackmail works. Get the goods on them, and make them pay."

Alexandra gave up pleading and buried her teeth in Drake's shoulder. He yelled a string of curses, then slapped her so hard her brain seemed to rattle in her skull. "Pull another stunt like that, hellcat, and I'll strangle you before Olivia gets a chance to shoot you."

But there were no more chances for any kind of stunt. They were on the deck now, and Olivia was waiting, gun in hand.

"Take her to the edge, Drake."

"Don't do it, Olivia," Alexandra pleaded. "You won't get away with this. You'll end up in jail like Louis did, but you'll be there the rest of your life."

"I will get away with it. I've already been to your apartment. You kept changing the lock, but I just kept getting new keys made. You shouldn't leave your purse lying around the office at the day care. All I had to do was sneak the keys out long enough to get duplicates made.''

''Someone will find out you killed me.''

''No, my dear.'' Olivia smiled. ''Your luggage is gone from your apartment, and so are your clothes. No one will be surprised that you've run again. 'Poor Alexandra,' we'll all say. 'Too bad she couldn't get her life together.'''

Olivia was right. They would all believe she'd run away. Even Ben, and that hurt most of all.

Olivia pointed the gun at Alexandra's head, then moved it at the last second, pointing it at Drake and pulling the trigger. He lost his hold on Alexandra and slid into Puget Sound, turning the water red with his blood.

''This time I'll take no chances,'' Olivia said. ''There will be no one who can tie me to your death. Ask forgiveness for all your sins, Alexandra. Always ask forgiveness. And when I go back to town, I'll ask Father Michael to pray for you.''

''But Father Michael is...'' Alexandra stopped and stared at Olivia. She was smiling again, as if they were out for a day of boating. All this time, Alexandra had feared she was going mad, but it was Olivia who'd actually gone mad. She'd slid over the edge of sanity as surely as Drake had slid over the edge of the deck. As surely as Alexandra was about to drown in the depths of Puget Sound.

Even if she jumped before she was shot, she wouldn't have a chance, not with her hands and feet tied. She turned and stared at the water. It would be the last thing she'd see and feel and hear.

Only now she heard a different sound. A helicopter.

Nearby. And the sound of a boat motor. Olivia heard them, too. Alexandra could see the shock in her eyes.

"Don't shoot me yet, Olivia," she said, her voice shaky as she called on the woman's madness to save her. "I need time to ask forgiveness. Give me time to pray. It's the Christian thing to do."

"It's too late, Alexandra. It's just too late."

A sound like an explosion filled the air, and the gun went off as the boat lurched forwards. Alexandra fell into the water. It wrapped around her, cold, wet, suffocating. Yet it was the heat of the fire from so long ago that she felt as she fought the weight of the water and struggled to hold her breath.

As her strength gave out, her thoughts turned to Ben and Doug and the happiness she'd almost found before the nightmare claimed her for its own.

I love you, Ben. I should have told you that I love you.

CHAPTER SIXTEEN

BEN RAMMED *Doug's Delite* into the stern of Olivia's yacht, his aim perfect, though his insides were as turbulent as any storm the Northwest had ever seen. His eyes were pinned on Olivia and the pistol. He heard the thunderous crack of gunfire a split second after the splintering crash of the boats. And he saw Alexandra struggle for balance, then fall into the water.

He didn't hesitate or stop to think of his chances of finding her once she'd sunk below the surface. He just kicked off his shoes and dove in.

Swimming beneath the surface, he kept his eyes peeled for movement. He wouldn't be able to hold his breath long. Already his lungs felt as if they were being crushed by huge weights. He surfaced once, then went under again, fighting the panic.

He couldn't go up for air again, not until he had her. Every second counted. Time was her life. He kept swimming and searching as the pressure built inside him. His lungs burned as if someone were holding a torch to his chest.

It was her hair that caught his attention, floating like a clump of seaweed just below a string of tiny bubbles. She was sinking slowly, fighting the power of the water as best she could with her bound feet and hands.

Kicking his own feet to keep from sinking deeper,

he reached for her and caught hold of her blouse. He yanked her to him and cradled her in his left arm as he worked his way to the surface.

The second their heads broke free, she started coughing and spitting up water. He sucked in as much air as he could hold and started searching for help. Sure enough, it was there in the form of two coast-guardsmen who'd jumped from their helicopter to help in the rescue.

"If she's choking, she's breathing," one of them said, swimming towards them.

"And no blood, so the bullet must have missed its mark," Ben said.

The guardsman motioned to the pilot of the copter. "Let's get her up and get her out."

"I've got you, baby," Ben yelled over the whir of the copter. "We're going home."

Reluctantly Ben let go of her as the guardsmen fit her into a rope basket and the copter hoisted her to the deck of *Doug's Delite.* Ben swam to the ladder, climbed on board and rushed to be at her side when they took her from the basket.

Alexandra coughed again, then gave him a weak smile. "Who says doctors don't make house calls anymore?"

Relief coursed through him and he breathed his first steady breath since he'd started searching for Alex-andra. "How you doing, baby?"

"Hanging in there. How did you know how to find me?" she asked, her voice low and hoarse.

"Your phone call," he said as he took his knife and cut through the rope that bound her hands. "I heard the boat motor in the background and thought you might be on Olivia's boat. I called the marina and the young guy who works there verified that the boat was out, and that two women and one man had boarded it just before five.''

''I don't even remember getting on the boat. I was drugged.''

''Which explains why the guy at the marina said the pretty young redhead looked as if she'd done a little too much partying.''

''Is that how you knew I was in trouble?''

''That, added to what we knew about Olivia's possible connection to the stolen cross and some new information Hannah told me when she realized you were with Olivia.''

''I still don't know how you found me in miles of open water.''

''Deciding you were heading towards San Juan Island was nothing short of a miracle. The coast guard did the rest. Their helicopter zeroed in on Olivia's boat.''

''And once we did, Dr. Jessup burned up the water getting to you,'' the older guardsman said. ''I wouldn't want to have to race him. He beat our boat by—'' he glanced at his watch ''—fifteen minutes and ten seconds. That's our boat coming there.'' He pointed to a cutter a few yards away. ''Just in time to give your abductress a nice escorted ride to jail.''

''Where is Olivia now?'' Alexandra asked.

''Standing at the bow of her ship, securely cuffed to a new friend,'' Ben said, cutting through the last shred of rope from Alexandra's ankles. ''Although I can't imagine why she was trying to kill you.''

''It's a long, long story,'' Alexandra said.

''Then let's save it. Right now I just want to make sure you're really all right.''

"We can airlift her in to see a doctor," the older guardsman said.

Alexandra shook her head. "I have my own doctor."

"Are you sure?" Ben asked. "It's going to take us a while to get back to the marina."

"I'm sure, Dr. Jessup. I'm very, very sure."

BEN HAD WANTED to take Alexandra straight to the hospital to have her checked out completely before she had to start dealing with the hours of police questioning that were sure to follow. But she insisted on one stop first. Room 1188 of Seattle Memorial Hospital.

"All indications are that my father died in the fire that night, but I can't let go of the belief that Gary Devlin and Jonathan Webber are the same person."

"I'd never ask you to. There comes a time when you have to go with your heart and your gut instinct. If I hadn't done that today, you'd be dead."

Dead. It hurt to say the word. But it would have hurt a million times more if he hadn't been in time to save her. He took Alexandra's hand and squeezed it, then dropped it when he saw Ernie Brooks standing over Devlin's hospital bed.

"What are you doing here?" he asked, not bothering to hide his irritation.

"Visiting an old friend."

"You come to town, and your friend gets the crap beat out of him. You're not a very lucky guy to have around."

"I didn't have anything to do with Gary getting beat up. I did my damage to him a long time ago."

"Then you're probably fortunate he doesn't remember it."

"I understand your doubts about me, Dr. Jessup. You're right on target. I'm here to clear my own conscience. Nothing I have to say is going to change the past, but I'm going to say it anyway, if Miss Webber wants to hear it."

Alexandra put a hand on Ben's arm as if to silence him. "Just tell me one thing, Ernie. Is Gary Devlin my father?"

"Yes, he is."

Alexandra all but fell into Ben's arms. He held her tight as tears slid down her cheeks. But this time he was certain they were tears of joy.

ALEXANDRA SAT by her father's bed and held his frail hand while Ernie Brooks spun a tale of danger and intrigue. The selling of sensitive Eagle Aerotech software to foreign countries was a very profitable business, and there were go-between agents who'd kill to make sure it didn't stop. At least, that was what the FBI had deduced when one of their top agents was killed while investigating the case.

That's when they'd gone to Jonathan Webber and invited him in on the action. He'd been certain that no one in his company was involved, and he'd been crushed when the evidence started piling up against Louis Kinard.

At that point, Seattle had held nothing for Jonathan. He and Carrie were getting a divorce, and she was going to take Alexandra and move back to Montana. His best friend in the whole world would be in jail for selling out the company they'd started together.

So, reluctantly, Jonathan had agreed to the FBI's offer of witness protection.

When he'd gotten his wife and daughter out of the house that night and was convinced they were safe, he'd pretended to walk back into the burning home, but instead had slipped behind the house, disappeared behind the shrubbery and climbed into the car that was waiting to take him away.

"How do you know it happened that way?" Alexandra asked, still struggling to understand.

"Because I'm the man who was driving the car that night."

"But why didn't he come back for me when he realized my mother was dead? Why did he just abandon me?"

"That almost killed him, Alexandra. You have to believe that. I was there when he found out, and watched him sob his heart out while he clung to a lifeless doll, the only thing he had left of you."

"He could have come back then. I needed him so."

"He didn't think you did. He knew you'd have a safe, happy home with Carrie's family. And we all still believed that his life was in danger from the agents who'd been cashing in on the sale of the software, and that if he came back for you, yours would be, as well. They were not the type of people who forgive and forget. He did what he thought was right, even if it broke his heart. That's why I had to come to Seattle now, why I finally had to tell you the truth."

"Does the FBI know you're here?"

"They do now. The permission just came through channels allowing me to level with you, but even if they hadn't, I would have. You deserved to know.

And Jonathan deserves to spend these last few years with the daughter he loved so much."

"Only he won't even know me. Even if he gets over this, his memories are lost."

"I know. And I'm sorry." He buried his hands in his pockets and rattled his keys nervously. "I've got to get out of here. I've done all I can do."

She nodded. "Thanks for telling me this. It's years too late, but I'm still glad I know."

Ernie stepped closer to the bed and put a hand on Jonathan's arm. "I doubt you can hear me, but if you can, you take care, old buddy. And if you're ever in Texas, look me up. We'll grab a beer and *not* talk about old times."

Ben crossed the room and took Alexandra in his arms. She held on tight and cried. For all she'd lost. And for all she'd gained. But mostly just for being alive and in the room with two men. One she'd loved forever. The other she'd only begun to love. But there was one more man in her life.

"Where's Doug?"

"Oh, no. He's still at the day-care center. Whoever's in charge is going to kill me."

"Don't worry. I know one of the owners."

They rushed out hand-in-hand. There were still questions, still problems to be faced, a million hurdles to overcome, but for the first time in her life, Alexandra felt as if she could handle them all.

Ben stopped walking, took her in his arms and spun her around in front of a half dozen nurses.

"What was that for?" she asked, still caught up in his arms.

"Just because I can, Alexandra Webber. Just because I can."

EPILOGUE

Two weeks later

BEN STOOD at the front door and greeted the guests as they arrived for a party to welcome Jonathan Webber home from the hospital and back into their lives. Helen and Louis Kinard. Their son, Drew, and his wife. Kenneth Richards. Hannah, Jack and Adam McKay. Even Katherine had flown in for the event. And, of course, Alexandra.

She was with her father now, walking him through the house that was so very much like the one he'd lived in twenty-one years ago. It had been a rough go for Jonathan the past two weeks, but he'd recovered well from the attack and had occasional lucid moments. He seemed especially alert tonight, perhaps because he was surrounded by family and old friends.

Olivia had been formally charged with the murder of Father Michael Cleary, the murder of Drake Phillips and the attempted murder of Alexandra. Charges had not been made concerning her role in the Eagle Aerotech crimes, in having Jonathan Webber attacked or running Debbie North off the road, but evidence was building against her in those deaths, as well.

The story was gradually being pieced together. It seemed that Olivia had come to the Webber home at Jonathan's insistence. Apparently the two of them argued about something written on the piece of paper that Jonathan had been holding over the lit candle. She'd meant to shoot him but instead shot Father Cleary when he'd jumped into the path of the bullet. Then she'd gone back to the church with a bleeding and wounded Father Cleary. She'd killed him to keep him from implicating her in the fire, then taken the cross and the money in his pockets to make it look like a robbery.

At present, she was in the hospital undergoing a complete psychiatric evaluation. Ben had an idea that she'd be there for quite a while.

But even with Olivia's black deeds hanging over them, it was a monumental night. Jonathan Webber, Louis Kinard and Kenneth Richards were together again. Louis Kinard had been cleared of all charges in connection with the Eagle Aerotech crimes, and Alexandra was reunited with her father.

Ben had good news to share, as well, though not as grand as what he'd hoped for. He'd planned to announce his engagement to Alexandra, but he couldn't. He hadn't asked her yet. The ring had been in his pocket for over a week, but every time he started to ask, he got cold feet. Not because he was afraid of marriage, but because he knew she was still reeling from all she'd been through, and he couldn't bear it if her answer was no.

LOUIS SAW Jonathan and Kenneth standing on the back deck. Kenneth was talking, but Jonathan was just staring into the distance. He was so different from the man Louis remembered. Then he'd been a dynamo, a real scrapper, tough and independent as they came. College roommate, business partner, best friend. Jonathan had meant the world to him. It was difficult accepting that Jonathan had believed him guilty of the Aerotech crimes. Not only believed him guilty, but had helped send him to prison.

If Louis had known that at the time, he'd have probably hated Jonathan for the betrayal. But it was difficult to hate a man in Jonathan's condition. Besides, they'd all made mistakes, and with Olivia's trial, the few secrets that remained among the three families would likely be plastered across the front pages of the Seattle newspapers and blared from radio and TV news programs. The blitz had already started.

Perhaps it was better this way. Lies ate away at you if they never came out. Devoured a man the way a cancer did. His only regret was that innocent people always had to be hurt.

He stepped onto the deck. "Hello, Jonathan."

Jonathan turned and their eyes met. "Hello, Louis."

It was the first time he'd called him by name, the first time he'd seen Jonathan without the blank stare. "I'm glad you're back. I've missed you."

"You were in prison," Jonathan said.

"Yeah. I was, but I'm out now." Louis took a deep breath and tried to find the words he wanted to say. "We used to be really good friends, Jonathan."

"We were friends?"

"Very good friends. We owned a business together."

"We didn't stay friends," Jonathan said, speaking slowly as if he were trying to get a handle on the relationship.

"No, but I'd like to give it another try."

"Yeah. Another try."

Louis pulled Jonathan into a bear hug. He didn't know how much Jonathan actually understood, but it was a start, and it felt good. But it wasn't enough.

"I really need to talk to you tonight, too, Kenneth."

"You don't owe me any explanations about anything, Louis, if that's what you're thinking."

"But I do. I don't know how to say this. It goes so far back."

"If you're talking about the affair you had with Olivia, that's old news."

"How long have you known about that?"

"Since right after it happened."

"It wasn't actually an affair. It was only a one-time thing, but I should never have let it happen."

"No, but you did."

"Did Olivia tell you?"

"Not in words, but I could read it in her actions. Thinking back, she probably wanted me to know."

"I don't know how I let her get to me that night. If I could undo any one night in my life, that would be it."

"I was taken in by her more than anyone," Kenneth admitted. "I not only believed her lies about her past, I believed for a long time that she loved me. Jonathan may have been the first one to learn the truth."

"What makes you think that?"

"My guess is that's why Olivia had the gun pointed at Jonathan the night of the fire. The paper he held over the candle was likely proof of the affair. He was probably insisting that she tell me the truth."

"That would be like Jonathan," Louis agreed. "He

always hated a lie. And then he'd had to give up his own daughter to live one.''

''All because I brought Olivia into our lives. I just hope this doesn't all come out during the trial, but if it does, we'll handle it.''

Most of all Kenneth hoped that the fact that Hannah was Louis's daughter and not his, never came out. He'd always feared that information might destroy his relationship with Hannah. He didn't believe that anymore. Hannah was made of stronger stuff than that. Still, all three families had been through enough heartache. It was time for the healing to begin.

But no matter what happened, Hannah was his daughter in every way that counted and he loved her more than life itself. He always would. Giving birth to Hannah might be the only worthwhile thing Olivia had ever done. He'd always be thankful to her for that, even though at the time her pregnancy had been quite a shock, since the news came right after his doctor had told him that medical tests had shown him to be sterile.

''We're friends,'' Jonathan said, breaking into the conversation. ''All of us. Friends.''

''You got it,'' Kenneth agreed. ''Webber, Kinard and Richards. Friends to the end.''

Helen joined them on the deck. ''How's it going?'' she asked, her voice soft and concerned.

''Pretty good,'' Louis said. ''Let's take a walk through Ben's gardens.''

''You were never one to notice flowers.''

''Maybe I just want to be alone with the prettiest woman at the party.'' He led her to a bench beneath the shade of a maple tree and tugged her down beside him. ''I've always loved you, Helen.''

"I know that."

He called on all the courage he had, determined to say what he had to say and get it over with once and for all. "But I wasn't always faithful."

"You don't need to do this, Louis."

"I do. I should have done it long go."

"Is this about the night you spent with Olivia?"

"You knew, too?"

"A wife always knows. But just in case I didn't, Olivia threw out enough hints that I couldn't have missed it if I'd wanted to."

"You never said a word."

"I was too hurt at first. Later it didn't seem to matter. I loved you and I knew you loved me and our children. We had a great marriage. I wasn't going to let a one-time mistake take that away from us."

"You're pretty wonderful."

"I know."

He kissed his wife, certain that in all the years they'd been together, and all they'd been through, he'd never loved her more.

"IT'S A GREAT PARTY," Jack said just before devouring yet another shrimp canapé.

"It is," Hannah agreed. "It's nice to see my dad talking and laughing with Louis. I know he missed him when Louis was in prison."

Jack kissed the back of her neck as he circled her with his arms and rested his hands on the swell of her belly. "You've handled this well, little mother. I was afraid the truth about Olivia would do you in."

"I wasn't sure how I'd feel about my mother, either. I thought I might hate her, but I don't. I hate what she's done, though, and I'll never feel the same about her. Mostly I just pity her that she let her need for money and recognition control her entire life until she didn't have an ounce of decency left."

"I can say one good thing about her," Jack said. "She has a terrific daughter."

"Thank you, sir. Now we better move into the living room. I think Ben Jessup's about to give a speech."

"I'D LIKE TO WELCOME all of you to the Jessup household," Ben said. "It's a thrill for me, and I know for you, as well, to have Jonathan Webber home from the hospital and back into the fold."

The room erupted in applause. Jonathan smiled and clapped along with them.

"And now I think we should hear from the woman who found Jonathan in the Seattle underground and brought him into the light."

Alexandra stepped to the front of the group. "I just want to say how proud I am to be Jonathan's daughter. I don't remember a lot about the first six years of my life, but I know they must have been filled with love. That love eventually brought both Dad and me back to Seattle, and back to each other."

Her eyes grew moist. "I'm thrilled to have my father back in my life, but I want more of him. I want to share the parts of his life that belonged to Gary Devlin, as well. I plan to try and find the family he had after he remarried. And if they'll let us, we'll be one happy family. And, of course, there'll be room for all of you."

Tears were rolling down her cheeks when she finished talking. Ben wanted to take her in his arms, but Katherine and Hannah got to her first. The three best friends threw their arms around one another, hugging and crying together.

Louis and Kenneth each got up and said a few words. And finally it was Ben's turn. He'd spoken in front of much larger groups than this many times in his life, but never had he been as nervous as he was right now.

JONATHAN WAS HANGING IN there, sitting on Ben's caramel-and-navy-striped sofa and occasionally clapping along with the others. Alexandra walked over to stand behind him as Ben started his speech.

"I know I'm a newcomer to this group, but I'd like to make an announcement that affects the three families represented here. The paperwork has begun for me to purchase Forrester Square Day Care. I promise to keep up the great work started by Katherine, Hannah and Alexandra. I'm smart enough to know I can't do that by myself, but I'm fortunate to have Alexandra agree to stay on to oversee the operation of the day care and to help establish a satellite program at Seattle Memorial Hospital."

The applause began again.

"I guess that's it—almost." The room grew quiet. "Alexandra, could you come up here and join me?"

Apprehension jumped along her nerve endings. She had no idea what Ben was going to do or say next, and surprises in her life had never turned out well. Her steps were hesitant as she walked to the front of the group. Ben took her hand and tugged her closer.

"I need you up here, too, Doug."

Doug came running to the front of the room and wrapped his sturdy arms around his dad's leg.

"I'm probably doing this all wrong, but to tell you

the truth, I'm scared to death, and I need all the moral support I can get.'' He turned back to Alexandra and took both of her hands in his. ''I had a little speech planned, but I can't remember a word of it, so I'll just have to say this plain. I love you, Alexandra, so much that I can't imagine spending my life without you. So...'' He reached into his pocket and pulled out a gold band with one very large marquise-cut diamond. ''Will you marry me—and Doug?''

Alexandra just stood there, tears wetting her eyes, her heart so full she thought it might burst into a million sparkling pieces. She met Ben's gaze and saw the love—and fear. He actually thought she might say no. For a brilliant doctor, he really didn't have a clue.

''Yes, I'll marry you.'' She wanted to say more, but a lump of pure joy filled her throat.

Ben took her in his arms and kissed her while her friends and father applauded and yelled out their approval, and Doug wrapped his arms around both of them.

Ben slipped the ring on her finger. ''I love you and I want you to share my life forever.''

''Forever,'' she agreed.

And this time the word didn't frighten her at all. The past was finally behind her. The nightmare was over. And all the dreams she'd never dared to dream were about to come true.